The
Beautiful
Avengers

Lara: the chic jetsetter schemed to smash Nick Bassolino's Hollywood romance by luring him from the bed of an aging star—into her own.

Beth: the idealistic hippie would play nursemaid to Frank Bassolino's children, then tempt him with her virginal beauty into a brutal confrontation with his wife.

Rio: the six-foot-plus porno star would tantalize and tease playboy Angelo Bassolino into impotence and disaster.

★

It was Omerta—a sexual revenge, but it became a bloody battle, a violent climax that blew the Bassolino family empire into oblivion.

☆   ☆

"Jackie Collins books are like midsummer Houston weather: hot and steamy. Her ten books contain enough overheated sex and action that if she writes any more like them the polar ice caps may be in danger of meltdown."

—*Houston Post*

Novels by Jackie Collins

Chances
The Love Killers
Lovers & Gamblers
The World Is Full of Divorced Women

Published by
WARNER BOOKS

THE
LOVE
KILLERS

(Originally titled: *Lovehead*)

Jackie Collins

WARNER BOOKS

A Warner Communications Company

The characters and locations in this novel are fictional. Any resemblance to the famous, infamous, known, and unknown is purely coincidental.

WARNER BOOKS EDITION

Copyright © 1974 by Jackie Collins Lerman
All rights reserved. This book or parts thereof may not be reproduced in any form without permission in writing.

This Warner Books Edition is published by arrangement with the author.

Warner Books, Inc.
666 Fifth Avenue
New York, N.Y. 10103

 A Warner Communications Company

Printed in the United States of America

First Warner Books Printing: July, 1975

Reissued: July, 1986

15 14

Chapter 1

'I don't care if you can't do anything else. I don't care if you lose your income, your home, your possessions. Fuck all of it, baby. Just gather up your self-respect and walk right out of it. To be a prostitute is to be a nothing, a mere tool of man. Take no notice of your pimps, your bosses. *We* will help you. *We* will give you all the help we can. *We* will get you so together that your old life will seem like a bad dream.'

Margaret Lawrence Brown had been speaking for fifteen minutes, and she paused to sip from a glass of water handed to her on the makeshift podium. The crowd which had come to hear her talk was gratifyingly large. They swelled around a huge area of Central Park, mostly women, a few men scattered amongst them.

Margaret spoke in a strong, outright voice. She didn't falter for words. The message she was giving came across loud and clear.

She was a tall woman of about thirty. No make-up, a strong radiant face, long black hair. She wore denims, boots, love beads. A cult figure in America. Everyone had heard of her.

She was a ceaseless campaigner for women's rights, and had won many a victory. She appeared on television constantly and had written three books. She had made a great deal of money, all of which she used for her organisation—F.W.N.—Free Women Now.

Everyone had laughed when she had taken up the cause of the prostitute. But they weren't laughing now, not after three months, not after thousands of women appeared to be giving up their chosen profession and following Margaret.

'You've got to get it together now!' Margaret screamed.

'Yeah!' the women screamed back.

'You're going to live again, you're going to come alive!'

'Yeah! Yeah!' The reaction from the crowd was gospel in its intensity.

'You're going to be *free* . . .'

'Yeah!'

Margaret slumped to the ground while the crowd still stamped and shouted its approval.

Blood spurted out of her head from a small, neat hole.

It was minutes before the crowd realised what had happened, before hysteria and panic set in.

Margaret Lawrence Brown had been shot.

The house in Miami could be approached only by going through electronically controlled gates, and then passing the scrutiny of two uniformed guards with pistols stuck casually in their belts.

Alio Marcusi passed this scrutiny easily. He was a fat, old man, with liquid booze-filled eyes and the walk of a pregnant cat.

He approached the big house humming softly to himself, uncomfortable in his too-tight grey check suit, sweating from the heat of a perfect, cloudless day.

A girl answered his ring at the door. A surly, big-limbed Italian girl, she spoke little English, but she nodded at Alio and told him that Padroni Bassalino was by the pool.

He patted her on the bottom, and made his way through the house to the patio which led on to an olympic-size swimming pool.

Mary Ann August greeted him. An exceptionally pretty girl, with old-fashioned, bee-hived blonde hair, and an incredible body exhibited in a small white bikini.

'Hi, there,' she said with a giggle, lifting herself off a lounging mat. 'I was just gonna make

myself a little drinkie. Want one?' She posed
herself provocatively in front of him, toying
with a gold chain which hung between her
mammoth breasts.

Alio contemplated her, licking his lips in
anticipation of the day—not far off, surely—
when Enzio would grow tired of her and pass
her on like all the others.

'Yeah, I'll have a Barcardi, plenty of ice. And
some potato chips, some nuts, a few black
olives.' He patted his large stomach sorrow-
fully. 'I had no time for lunch today. Such a
busy day. Where is Enzio?'

Mary Ann gestured out towards the never-
ending gardens.

'He's out there somewhere pruning his roses
I think.'

'Ah, yeah, his roses.' Instinctively Alio
glanced back at the house, and sure enough she
was there, Rose Bassalino, peering out through
a chink in her curtains.

Rose, Enzio's wife. She hadn't left her room
for fifteen years, and the only people she would
talk to were her three sons. She kept up an
endless vigil at her window, waiting and
watching.

Mary Ann wiggled over to the bar and
started preparing the drinks. She was nineteen
years old and had lived with Enzio Bassalino
for six months—something of a record.

Alio settled in a chair and slowly closed his
eyes. Such a very busy day . . .

'Hey, ciao, Alio, my friend, my boy. How you feeling?'

Alio woke with a start and jumped guiltily up.

Enzio loomed over him. Sixty-nine years old, but with the hard, bronzed body of a man half his age, sharp white teeth, a craggy, strong, lined face, topped by thick steel-grey hair.

'I feel good, Enzio, I feel fine.' They clasped hands, fondled backs. They were cousins, and Alio owed everything he had to Enzio.

'You want a drinkie, sweetheart?' Mary Ann enquired, nestling her body against Enzio's back, rubbing herself against him.

'No,' he dismissed her quickly, 'go in the house. I'll ring if I want you.'

Mary Ann didn't argue, she quickly went. Perhaps that was why she had lasted longer than the others.

'Well?'

'It is done,' Alio replied, 'I saw it myself. A masterful job, one of Tony's boys. He was gone before anyone knew what happened. I flew straight here.'

Enzio nodded thoughtfully. 'There is no greater satisfaction for a man than a perfect hit. This Tony's boy, pay him an extra thousand and watch him. A man like that could deserve promotion. A public execution is not an easy job.'

'No, it's not,' Alio agreed, sucking on a black olive.

9

* * *

'She must be thirty,' the woman hissed.

'Of course, she must be,' the other woman agreed.

Lined, and over made-up, the two middle-aged women watched Lara Crichton climb out of the Marbella Club pool. She was a perfectly beautiful girl of twenty-six. Thin, sun-tanned, with rounded sensual breasts, a mane of sun-streaked hair that only the very rich seem to be able to cultivate.

She lay on a mat next to Prince Alfa Masserini and sighed loudly. 'I'm getting bored with this place, darling, can we go somewhere else?'

Prince Alfa leapt quickly up. 'Why are you bored?' he demanded, 'am *I* boring you? Why should you be bored when you are with me?'

Lara sighed again. He *was* getting impossibly boring. But who else was there? Lara never let go of anyone until there was someone else firmly ensconced in his place. She had been through most of the Princes and Counts who were available, and a few movie actors, and a Lord or two. It really was tiresome that one had set oneself such a high standard.

'I don't understand you, Lara,' Prince Alfa was still moaning, 'no woman has ever told me she was bored with me. I am not a boring man, I am vibrant, lively, I am—how you say—the life and brains of the party.'

Lara noticed with an even heavier sigh that

as he spoke he was getting an erection in his tight white Cerrutti silk shorts.

'Oh, God, do shut up,' she muttered under her breath. Sex was becoming the biggest bore of all. So predictable, so worked out, so mechanical.

'Come,' aware of his erection, and proud, Prince Alfa was pulling her to her feet. 'First we take a little rest,' he winked, 'then we take the Ferrari up in the mountains, a little drive, a mix amongst the peasants.'

'All right.' Reluctantly Lara allowed herself to be pulled up. All eyes followed them as they left.

They had separate suites, but by agreement all sexual activity was in Lara's. She stopped him from coming in.

'What's the matter?' he protested, 'I have a good hard-on—a *very* good one.'

'Save it till later,' Lara said softly, she hoped kindly. 'I will rest and call you when I wake up.' She closed the door on his protests.

She felt restless and hemmed in. A feeling she had often felt when married to Michael Crichton. A divorce had solved the feeling then, what now?

The phone rang. She picked it up, her voice firm, ready to tell Alfa no—definitely no. But it was New York calling.

'Yes?' Lara wondered who even knew she was here.

Jackie Collins

'Lara? Lara, is that you? This is such a bad line.'

'Who is that?'

'Lara, can you hear me? This is Cass. Something terrible has happened. Margaret has been shot. They've shot Margaret.'

Chapter 2

Margaret Lawrence Brown was rushed to the nearest hospital. She was still alive, but barely. Her loyal followers gathered in tight, silent groups.

The closest to her were allowed in the hospital, where they waited with as much hope as they could muster. There were no tears, Margaret would have hated that. Cass Long and Rio were perhaps the closest to her.

Cass was her secretary, confidante, organiser, protector. They had been at college together.

Rio Java was Margaret's most famous supporter, and a close friend. An underground movie star with four children and no husband or even a steady man in her life, she was a staunch and founder member of F.W.N.

They stood together near to the door of the Emergency Room. A doctor had just announced they were doing a blood transfusion.

'Where's Dukey?' Rio asked.

'He's on his way,' Cass replied, her face white.

They watched silently as more doctors appeared and went into the room.

'Can I *see* her?' Cass pleaded as one doctor emerged.

'Are you a relative?' he asked kindly, noting Cass's bloodsoaked dress. She had cradled Margaret's head on her lap until the ambulance arrived.

'Yes,' Cass lied.

The doctor held her arm. 'It's not a pretty sight.'

Cass bit her lip to stay silent.

'Well, I suppose if you're a relative. Of course it's against regulations but—all right.'

Rio nodded at Cass to go ahead, and she followed the doctor into the room.

They were doing everything they could. Two catheters were allowing the first pint of blood to be transfused. A tube was at her nose. A doctor was working at massaging her heart.

'There's not much hope, is there?' Cass asked blankly. The doctor shook his head and led her quietly out.

'Oh Christ, who can have done such a thing?' Cass asked. She had been asking that same question ever since the moment in the park when Margaret fell.

In her mind she had considered the possibilities. Margaret had many enemies, a lot of people were jealous of her, they were jealous of the position she held, the fact that she was still young and extremely attractive, the causes she fought for. They were also jealous of the fact that she led her life exactly as she pleased, and didn't give a damn about being criticised or gossiped about. The man she was currently living with was Dukey K. Williams, a black Soul Singer with a dubious and violent past.

Cass didn't like him. She felt that he was using Margaret.

Cass knew of all the hate mail Margaret received. 'Nigger Lover', 'Commie Whore', and the suchlike. There were also the threats to kill her.

'Lawrence Brown. I saw you on the *Johnny Carson Show* the other night. I hate you, you look like a rat. I hope you drop dead. I might kill you myself.'

These letters were almost a daily occurrence, so mundane as to be immediately ignored. The ones that had always worried Cass were the telephone threats. The muffled voices warning Margaret to leave certain causes alone. Recently it had been the matter of the prostitutes. So many had been following Margaret that suddenly the pimps, the madames, the certain branch of hoods that controlled it all, were getting worried. A dearth of prostitutes, it was getting to be an impossible situation, and each time Margaret held one of her open-air speeches hundreds more vanished overnight, spurred on by the fact that F.W.N. offered them more than words, it offered them a concrete chance of starting afresh. The organisation arranged jobs, living accommodations, even money if the need was urgent.

There had been many threats for Margaret to drop the 'Great Hooker Revolution' as *New Month* Magazine called it. They had recently featured her on their cover, with a six-page story inside.

Dukey K. Williams arrived as soon as he could. He had been at a recording session.

There was a struggle to get in the hospital. The place was swarming with police, press, and television crews.

Dukey, accompanied by his manager and pressman, refused any comment. He pushed his way through the mob, and was finally stopped by a police security man who would not grant him permission to board the lift.

'Oh, for God's sake,' Dukey said, 'get the bastard out of my way or I'll smash him in two.'

The cop glared, and his hand twitched nervously near his gun.

'Calm down, Dukey,' his manager said

quickly, 'they're only protecting Margaret. Cass must be up there.'

Eventually Cass was sent for, and the cop was persuaded to let him through.

'How did it happen?' Dukey asked quickly, 'have they caught anyone? Will she make it?'

'They don't seem to know,' Cass said quietly, 'it doesn't look good.'

Rio was at the lift to meet them. 'Forget it,' she said shortly, 'Margaret just died.'

Chapter 3

Enzio Bassalino was a big and powerful man, and it always amused Mary Ann August when the mood took him to cook dinner. He would clear the kitchen of all the help, tie an apron around himself, then he would go to work cooking spaghetti, and garlic bread, and a special meat sauce '*à la Enzio*'.

'Honey—you look so *funny* in that apron,' Mary Ann trilled. She was allowed in the kitchen only as an onlooker. 'Don't you want little Mama to help you?'

Little Mama was the name Enzio called her. She was unaware of the fact that it had also been the name of every girl before her.

'No,' Enzio shook his head, 'you fetch me some more *vino*.'

Mary Ann obliged, and perched on the kitchen table swinging her long legs. She was wearing an extremely tight black dress, cut very low at the front. Enzio chose all her clothes, and they were always of the same style. She was not allowed to wear trousers or shirts or anything casual. She didn't mind. Life was certainly a lot better being with Enzio than it had been before, and she catered to his every need. After all, Enzio Bassalino was a famous man, a man she was thrilled and honoured to be with.

'Taste this,' proudly Enzio offered her a spoonful of the steaming, rich meat sauce.

She opened her mouth dutifully. 'Ouch, noonzi, that's hot!' She pouted, 'You've burnt your little Mama . . .'

Enzio roared with laughter. He was celebrating. Tonight he would laugh at anything.

'You're mean,' Mary Ann had lapsed into baby talk, 'why you so mean to your rickle lickle girlie?'

'You don't even know what being mean is,' Enzio said, dipping his finger in the boiling hot sauce, licking, approving, adding more wine. 'You're a nice little kid. Stay that way and you'll be all right.'

In his own peculiar way he was quite fond of Mary Ann. She was dumber than most broads, and never asked any questions. And stacked just the way he liked, and obliging. Nothing was ever too much trouble. He was sick to death of the usual routine. They moved in with you, and within weeks they thought they owned you. They asked questions, and got nosey, and even sometimes complained of a headache when he wanted to make love. Enzio was very proud of the fact that even now, aged sixty-nine, he could still get it up once or twice a week. Sometimes he thought with pleasant nostalgia about the time it had been once or twice or even three or four times a night. What a man he had been! What a giver of pleasure!

Now it was up to his sons to carry on the Bassalino tradition with women. And he had three of them, three fine young men of whom he was more than proud. They were his life. Through them the name of Bassalino would be carried on. And when he became old, really old, they would be there to protect him as he had protected them.

It was a good job they had not taken after their mother. Rose was mad as far as Enzio was concerned, locked up in her room, spying, looking, only speaking to her sons when they visited. She had been there for fifteen years, fifteen years of trying to break Enzio's back, trying to make him feel the guilt.

But he refused to. Let her be the one to suffer. What he did in his life was his business, and she had no right to try and interfere.

In his heyday Enzio Bassalino had acquired the nickname of The Bull. This was on account of his habit of mounting every agreeable female who crossed his path. Sometimes they weren't so available, and while dallying with the wife of a friend of his known as Vincent the Hog, he received his one and only bullet wound. 'Right up the ass,' the story went. 'Vincent the Hog caught them at it and shot him right up the ass.'

Fortunately for Enzio that story wasn't strictly true. Vincent the Hog had shot him all right, but the bullet had landed in a fleshy part of his posterior and had not caused any real damage. Enzio was not pleased, and Vincent the Hog had then suffered a series of mishaps that had started with his house burning down, and ended with him being fished out of the river on the other end of a concrete block. Enzio didn't take kindly to ridicule, and the story of him being shot had caused many an unwelcome snigger.

Shortly after that incident he met and married Rose Vacco Moran. She was the daughter of a friend. Thin, proud faced, with the fragile Madonna quality of a young Italian virgin. They had a huge wedding, a long feast. She wore white lace, and Enzio a shiny black morning suit, white shoes, gloves, a red carnation. Rose was eighteen. Enzio thirty-three.

They became a popular couple, Rose soon shrugging off her quiet upbringing and joining in the more flamboyant life style of her husband. She didn't wish to become a housewife, she didn't wish to stay at home and involve herself in cooking and children and church activities. She dutifully gave birth to their first son, but it was left at home with a nanny while she spent all her time out and about with Enzio.

He didn't mind, in fact he was flattered. Rose was becoming a beautiful, intelligent woman, and Enzio knew he was much envied. While other men left their wives at home and took their girlfriends to the racetracks, bars and clubs, Enzio brought Rose. She became one of the boys, their friend and confidante.

Enzio often marvelled at his luck in finding a woman like Rose. She satisfied him in every way, and presented him with a second son three years after the first.

He had no secrets from her. She knew all about his business activities, and as each year he grew more successful, took over more territory, knocked out more rivals, she was right there helping him. On more than one occasion she was at his side when he dealt out his form of justice to people who had double-dealed him. 'That Rose has more balls than a man,' Alio would tell everyone, 'she's one fine woman.'

She had many admirers, and Enzio knew it. It puffed him up with pride, she was his woman, and that was that.

Angelo, their third son, was born, and with the other two children, now nine and twelve, Rose decided she should spend more time at home. Enzio agreed. There was no point in her coming on the short trips to Chicago and the Coast. They had a beautiful house and it was right that Rose should stay with the children and enjoy it.

She persuaded him that they should enlarge their circle of friends. All their friends in some way or other were involved in the rackets, and Rose suddenly wanted different people around. There was an actor and his wife who had an estate close by, and Rose started inviting them over. A banking family came next, and then the Cardwells who lingered at the bottom of high society. Gradually Rose surrounded them with new people, and gradually the old faces were squeezed out.

Enzio didn't like it. His business trips became longer, he acquired a small apartment. He acquired a stream of whorish girlfriends. 'Dumb Heads' he called them. He still adored Rose. Why had she changed?

One night he returned home hours before she expected him. He wanted to surprise her, it was the week of their twenty-first wedding anniversary. He wanted to have a talk, quietly. He wanted to explain how he felt. He wanted their closeness back.

At thirty-nine Rose was still a fiercely attractive woman. The thick black hair, dark complexion, the figure that had aged sensuously.

She greeted him coldly. She wanted a divorce, she wanted to marry Charles Cardwell.

She knew all about her husband's apartment, his whores. She wanted to be free.

Enzio listened in amazement. Charles Cardwell was twenty-six years old, a layabout with no money.

Enzio was calm. Had she slept with him, he enquired? Yes, Rose replied. She never lied. She was never afraid.

Enzio agreed to her requests. She went to bed. Enzio made some phone calls and later that night Charles Cardwell was brought to the house.

He was a pale young man, obviously shaken and frightened of his escort—four of Enzio's most trusted lieutenants. He smiled weakly at Enzio. 'Now listen . . .' he began.

Enzio ordered his mouth taped, his arms tied.

They carried him up to Rose's bedroom. She woke quickly. She stared at the helpless figure of her lover, then her eyes shifted to Enzio. She shook her head, she knew Enzio's brand of justice.

He took her from the bed and held her so she couldn't move, only watch. And then the knives came out and Charles Cardwell was sliced to death in front of her.

Chapter 4

It had not been easy for Lara to extract herself from the Prince. They had been together for six months and he was very possessive, suspicious, and jealous.

When she told him that she had to leave immediately for New York, he jumped to the only conclusion that it was possible for his mind to reach.

'Who is he? What has he got to offer you that I cannot give you?'

'It's not a man,' Lara explained patiently, 'it's a family situation.'

'But you have no family, you always told me you have no family.'

Lara nodded. 'I know, but I have these distant relatives,' she paused, 'I have a step-sister called Beth, she needs me.'

'A step-sister,' Prince Alfa shouted, 'you can't just acquire a step-sister. I know it's a man, Lara, I know that . . .'

'Oh please. Think what you like. I have to leave and that's that.'

'I'll come with you.'

'I don't want you with me.'

They argued some more until at last he left. Lara finished packing, and almost relieved to be rid of him, she left for the airport.

Lara Crichton always got first-class service wherever she went. Young, beautiful, the ex-wife of one of the richest men in London, she was truly one of what the press referred to as 'the beautiful people'. Constantly featured in the glossy fashion magazines as a shining example of true femininity, she epitomised all that Margaret Lawrence Brown was against.

It would have been a journalistic scoop for someone to discover that they were in fact half-sisters, sharing the same father but different mothers.

For individual reasons, as each reached personal fame, they felt no need to admit the fact to anyone. They had been brought up in different countries, their whole lives were completely alien to each other. Occasionally they met, and there was a true warmth between them. A sort of love that crossed the very obvious differences between them, and they understood each other and never criticised the other's way of life.

Their father, Jim Lawrence Brown, had never married either of their mothers. Margaret was five when her mother died.

Jim had moved on, taking the child with him to California, where he met a married woman whose husband was away for a year. He moved in with her and eventually she gave birth to Lara. When her husband returned she gave the child and five thousand dollars to Jim, to move on . . .

With the money he bought an old car and trailer, which served as a sort of home. Margaret, at five, was almost in complete charge of Lara. Jim wasn't a bad father, but he was always in a dream, playing his guitar, sleeping. They went to Arizona and stayed on a farm, owned by a widow, Mary Chaucer.

Margaret started school. She was a very bright child, far advanced for her years.

Soon Jim started to get restless. He had been far too long in the same place, but he was tied by the children. Perhaps that was why he married Mary Chaucer. She was older than Jim, a plump, smiling lady, and looking back, Margaret could only imagine that he married her to give Lara and her some security, for he must have planned to move on. Exactly one month after the marriage, he left.

Margaret was nine. She found his note. It

was a coward's note, full of apologies, and five hundred dollars.

Later Mary gave birth to Jim's third daughter, Beth, a child he never even knew about.

After that things were different. With no man around work at the farm became slapdash and unorganised. Mary was tired and ill. The baby had worn her out. Money started to run short, as did the once smiling Mary's temper.

Margaret was sent off to a boarding school, and Lara to relatives of Mary's in England. They did not see each other for ten years, by which time Margaret was at college, and Lara was doing well as a model in London.

Beth was now ten and living with Mary in a small apartment. She went to school while Mary worked.

Margaret wanted to help them, but it was hard enough managing to pay for her own education. An education she was determined to have.

Lara had won a competition in a magazine, and the prize was a trip to Hollywood. At sixteen she was really beautiful, natural with none of the polish she later acquired. She was happy in England, in fact to Margaret she seemed almost completely English—accent and all. They spent a weekend together, and the closeness of their early years was there.

Time went by and they went their separate, highly individual ways. Occasionally they wrote or phoned. But if the need for contact was not there, there was a deeper bond of love and security.

Mary died of cancer when Beth was fifteen, and although both her sisters invited her to live with them, she preferred a more independent life, and she went off to live in a hippy commune with her boyfriend, Max.

Margaret didn't object. She was already launched on an equality for women project. Her first book *Women—The Unequal Sex* was about to be published. Her star was beginning to shine.

In London Lara met and married Michael Crichton—whose father was one of the richest men in Europe, and Michael his only heir.

The marriage lasted a year. Enough to establish Lara as a personality in her own right. *Women's Wear Daily* and *Vogue* hardly went to press without carrying her picture or some anecdote about what she was wearing, doing, or who she was being seen with.

The shooting of Margaret Lawrence Brown was headlines, but the photographers still turned out at Kennedy Airport to welcome Lara Crichton.

She posed briefly in her Yves Saint Laurent man's suit and big hat, her cool green eyes hidden behind fashionable large sunglasses, Gucci bracelets jangling alongside her black-faced Cartier watch.

'What are you here for, Miss Crichton?' asked a reporter anxiously.

'Business,' Lara replied, unsmiling, 'very personal business.'

There was a limousine waiting for her, and she sat back and relaxed. During the drive into New York Lara remembered in detail her last meeting with Margaret. She had been in New York for two days only to do some shopping. As usual Margaret invited her over. Lara had fitted the visit in between lunch at Pavilion and a leg-waxing session at Elizabeth Arden.

Margaret had greeted her in her usual outfit of blue jeans, faded shirt, the perennial blue tinted shades that helped her eyesight, her long hair unkempt, no make-up.

Lara tut-tutted. 'If you bothered,' she said, 'you could look ravishing.'

Margaret had laughed in her face. 'Do you realise how much time you waste plastering yourself with crap?'

'I'm getting a directorship of a big make-up concern,' Lara said firmly. 'I shall send you a crate of perfumes, lipsticks, glosses, all sorts of things.'

'Stuff it!' Margaret laughed. They both hated the way the other one looked. It was a friendly hate.

'So, what's happening?' Margaret had fixed her a drink, and they had sat down amongst the clutter in Margaret's apartment, and Lara had let it all come out. She always did with her sister, it was better than going to an analyst. She talked about her problems for an hour.

Was Prince Alfa the one? Should she sell some of her blue chips? What did Margaret think of her new emerald ring?

Boring small chat. Looking back Lara shuddered. She never asked Margaret about herself, she never bothered. How narrow she must have seemed to her sister, how selfish and completely involved with herself. And yet Margaret had always listened patiently as if she had all the time in the world.

Why was it you always found out how much you needed someone just when it was too late?

Chapter 5

Beth Lawrence Brown came to New York by train. It was the first time she had been there. In fact, the first time she had been anywhere outside of the commune which had been her home since she was fifteen. Now twenty, she was a clear-skinned, blonde girl, with hair that hung straight and thick and reached below her waist. She had never used make-up, and her face was almost childlike, with large blue eyes, and a wide, sensual mouth.

She wore her usual clothes, a long dress of some Indian design, patched in places, thonged sandals on bare feet, and many necklaces of thin leather with hand-painted beads and signs hanging from them. Close to her neck, almost a choker, there was a thin gold chain with a gold

cross. On the cross were engraved the words
LOVE—PEACE—MARGARET.

The two sisters had been very close—not in
terms of distance but in the same way that
Lara and Margaret were close, there was a
feeling of unity.

Beth carried with her a large suede, pouchy
bag. In it were her things—a hairbrush, a pair
of blue jeans, a shirt, and many books. She
didn't believe in possessions, her passion was
reading.

'You wanna buy me a drink, baby?' a drunk
sidled up to her, 'I'll give you a little action in
exchange.'

She ignored him, her face pensive and
thoughtful. Margaret would have told him to
fuck off out of it; Lara would have said what a
dreadful little man.

Cass had promised there would be someone
to meet her. She was supposed to wait at the
enquiry desk. But the train was early, and she
didn't want to hang around, so she decided to
walk to Cass's apartment.

She couldn't believe what had happened. It
seemed inconceivable that Margaret was dead.
She was such a good person, so clever. All right,
she was tough. Everyone knew she was tough,
but how else would she have survived in the
jungle she had chosen to work in.

Beth had last seen her six months previously. She arrived with Cass to stay for a
couple of days. Everyone at the commune liked

her, in fact they always welcomed her visits. She brought all the new books, record albums, and toys for the children—clever toys, not commercial junk. There were ten children living at the farm, and they were shared amongst the five women and eight men who lived there. One of them was Beth's, a little girl of four.

Margaret shared in the work whilst she was there. She didn't mind what she did, washing floors, helping cook, gardening. She said it helped her to relax.

They celebrated, before she left, with a party. Great sounds and great hash that Max had brought in from California. Margaret had gone off with Clasher because he was short and ugly and the least likely to be her choice. Sex was a very free thing; no hang-ups, no jealousies, no pressures.

When Margaret left the next morning she had given Beth the gold chain and kissed her and whispered, 'You're really lucky, you have the perfect life here.'

And Beth had smiled, a wide, childish smile, and made her promise to come back soon.

'After the summer,' Margaret had vowed.

Now the summer was just ending and Beth was in New York. She didn't know for how long, but she just felt it was where she should be.

* * *

Enzio took the call in his study. He smiled and nodded. Of course things were back to normal. He had been right. His decision had been the only way. Semi-retired he may be, but any major thing that had to be taken care of he was the one they all turned to.

Frank, his eldest son, had suggested other ways of dealing with the trouble. But what did Frank know? Thirty-six years old, a good businessman, but when it came to decisions his ideas were all soft.

What good were threats? Definite action like the old days was the only way.

Margaret Lawrence Brown had been dead two weeks, and the trouble had stopped. With no one to guide them, no leader to turn to, the prostitutes were quiet. It was almost as if with the killing of Margaret their fighting spirit had been killed also.

Slowly, girls who had vanished, taken other jobs, came drifting back. They seemed oblivious to the beatings and insults they faced. They seemed once more defeated.

Enzio was in a buoyant mood. He ordered a full-length Chinchilla coat for Mary Ann, and it arrived within hours. They celebrated on it. Mary Ann not sure of what they were celebrating but a willing partner in anything Enzio wanted to do.

'You are my great big Italian lover,' she purred, 'my big, big man.'

'And you are a hot, juicy little piece,' he replied laughingly, 'my favourite piece of lasagne!'

He liked to look at her, her blonde, curvy body, her amazing large breasts, her silky skin, her pouty mouth. It would be quite a while before he grew tired of this one.

Chapter 6

Lola was not the girl's real name. She was thin and scruffy, with city black eyes, and clothes that announced her as the hooker she was. She bit her nails all the time, hungry, nervous, little nibbles. Her arms told the story of her drug addiction. She was nineteen years old.

She had been beaten up. Not badly, a few bruises around her body, a cigarette burn on her backside. Just enough to make her aware of the fact that there was more to come.

She knew about it all. She had known about it before it happened. She lived with Charlie Mailer. Charlie was one of Tony's boys. Charlie had pulled the hit on Margaret Lawrence Brown.

Lola scurried down the street. It was the first

time she had been out since it happened, the first time she had dared.

She wore a short skirt, summer lace-up boots, tight sweater, long matted hair, spiky eyelashes. Charlie had kicked her out of bed— 'Get out and earn something, then maybe we'll catch a movie. Don't come back with less than a couple of hundred.'

She had huddled in bed for two weeks, and Charlie had not minded. Flushed with his own success, he had been out a lot. Tony was pleased with him. Tony wanted him around.

She knew that Charlie was ready to dump her. He was moving up, and he didn't want her hanging on. She didn't mind. She knew what she was going to do.

A man stopped her, pulled her by the arm. She shook herself free. 'Not tonight,' she said angrily, 'I'm not working tonight.'

She hurried on, occasionally glancing behind her, making sure she wasn't followed.

She had a piece of newspaper in her hand, an address. She stopped and peered at it.

'Where you going, girlie?' a passing drunk enquired.

'Piss off,' she snapped back.

When she found the address, she hesitated about going in. She stood on the pavement and gazed up at the building.

She thought about Susan, her little sister, and then she spat angrily on the pavement and marched right in.

'I want to see Cass Long,' she said. 'She's not expecting me, tell her it's urgent.'

The doorman looked her over. He was old and sour and his watery eyes stayed fixed to her legs while he buzzed Cass's apartment.

Cass told him to send the girl up. So many women had been to see her since Margaret's death, she was used to it. She gave them coffee and a chat, and a picture of Margaret inscribed 'Peace—Love'. In a way it was a solace to know how deeply so many people had cared.

Beth let Lola in, and took her in the kitchen to offer her refreshments. She knew by looking at her that she was a junkie.

'I don't want anything,' Lola said. 'I have something to say, so I'll make it short.'

Cass came in then. There were deep shadows under her eyes, she looked tired.

'I don't want the reward,' Lola said hurriedly. 'I don't want money, pity, anything. You can see what I am, it's no big secret. Margaret gave people hope, she wouldn't have gotten me together—I'm a loser—but I had a sister—just a kid. Oh shit—I don't even want to tell you about it.' She paused, wiped her nose on the back of her hand. 'One of Tony's boys did it—it doesn't matter who—he was working on orders—Tony was working on orders. The guy who wanted it done was Enzio Bassalino—he arranged it—the hit was *all* his. He lives in Miami. They say he's retired, but he controls it all—the words to kill her came out of his mouth—not out of the gun.'

Cass didn't say anything. She felt very strongly that the girl was speaking the truth.

'I've got to go now.' Lola started to leave.

'Will you speak to the police?' Cass asked.

'Nope,' Lola shook her head, 'it's a waste of time. Half of them are in Bassalino's pocket. If you want him you'll have to get him yourself.'

'I don't understand,' Cass said.

'Think about it. You could do it, you're clever, you have connections,' Lola shivered suddenly, she had more to do. 'Look, I can take care of the guy who did the hit—but the real murderer is Bassalino. I admired Margaret Lawrence Brown—just you get that fucker.'

'Can you wait?' Cass pleaded. She wanted to call Dukey or Rio, someone who would understand this whole thing better than she did.

Lola shook her head.

Outside it was dark, and Lola headed for Times Square. She didn't have to pull a trick, make a score. But somehow it seemed right that she did.

She stationed herself in the foyer of a movie house and approached the first man going in on his own.

He was middle-aged, with a throaty cough. They bargained and then walked quickly together to his hotel nearby. He insisted on going in first, alone, and she followed a few minutes later.

The room was small and poky, the bed unmade.

She started to undress, and the man told her to keep her boots on. He took nothing off, merely unzipped his trousers and shook himself free.

They started, and Lola stared unseeingly at the ceiling. She was calm and detached, she knew exactly what she was going to do.

He finished quickly and Lola took her money and left. She walked slowly home.

Charlie was asleep. She went in the kitchen and opened a coke and drank straight from the can. The cold bubbles hurt her throat. Then she reached on top of the fridge right to the back where Charlie kept his revolver. She checked it carefully. It was loaded. She fitted on the silencer. She knew a lot about guns.

She walked to the door of the bedroom and called his name. He wakened slowly, sat up, saw the gun she was pointing at him.

'What the f . . .' he began.

She shot him in the leg. The bullet made a satisfying soft thud.

He attempted to stand up. His face was a mask of anger and surprise. She shot him right between the legs, directly at his scrotum.

He screamed out in agonised pain.

She shot him through the heart. He fell to the floor and was silent.

She put the gun down beside him and left the apartment. She took the lift to the top, forty-five floors up and let herself out on to the roof. She didn't hesitate. She walked straight to the edge and threw herself over.

She was impaled on some railings and died in the ambulance on the way to the hospital.

Chapter 7

'It's settled then?' Rio asked. She stared around at the small gathering in her living room. 'Now I don't want anybody shitassing out of it. If we agree, it's right on, no backing out,' she stared directly at Lara, 'no getting bored and high-tailing off to some little jet-set paradise.'

Lara spoke quietly, but her face flushed. 'Listen, Rio, this isn't a game to me. Margaret was my sister, and different though we may have been, I loved her as much as any one of you. I know what I have to do, and believe me I'll do it very, very well.'

'Rio didn't mean anything,' Cass said quickly, 'we're all a bit uptight. Who wouldn't be after the last few weeks? Now it's settled and we've decided, well I think we'll all feel easier. I know I will.'

Dukey K. Williams stood up suddenly, his powerful frame menacing the room. 'I still think my way's best.'

'Your way!' Rio scoffed. 'Good morning Mr Big Boss Man Bassalino, I understand it was you who gave the order to shoot Margaret, well come here Mister Bad Man for I am going to beat you to a pulp with my big strong hands. Dukey, you're full of shit. This guy's a big-time gangster. If you got anywhere near him you'd get your ass blown off. And even if you could get to him—what then? Kill him? What's dead? Dead is nothing, man, dead is an easy scene. The way we've thought of is the only way to get at him—the *only* way.'

Dukey sighed. 'Rio, you live your life between your legs. A little bit of screwin' here, a little bit of ass there. So what? These guys have had it all before.'

'I can make it work,' Rio said confidently.

'Yeah, you probably can. A sex freak like you. Maybe Lara too, I'm not into her whole scene, but she looks like a heavy lady. But Beth? You've got to be kidding. A baby like her will be mashed up and eaten by the dudes you're talkin' about.'

Beth spoke up for herself. 'I can do it, Dukey,' she widened her soft, blue eyes. 'I want to do it.'

'It's settled,' Rio announced, 'fucking settled. And we start tomorrow.'

Dukey K. Williams left the meeting shortly afterwards.

'Son of a bitch!' he muttered under his breath, 'sonofabigblackbitch! Motherfuckers!' He climbed into his white Rolls-Royce parked illegally outside Cass's apartment house. In anger he shoved a tape into the stereo machine. It happened to be *Dukey K. Williams Sings Dukey K. Williams*. The first track was 'Soul, Grit and Margaret'. He had written it for her. What a stubborn woman she had been. One hell of a wildcat, in bed and out. If only she had listened to him . . .

'Drop it,' he had warned her time and time again, 'don't fuck around with the big boys. You save a few hookers, ain't gonna help. Save a few, lose a few, it's all shit.'

She had just smiled at him, that warm sexy Margaret smile, and ignored his advice.

He didn't know how it happened, but suddenly he was in the middle. Right in the fuckin' middle.

There was some money he owed, not a lot by his standards, a couple of hundred thousand. That was chicken feed to him really, he could pick that up on an album, a couple of weeks doing a gig in some Miami shithouse.

The thing was he owed it, and the way things were he just didn't have it on hand to pay back.

He had just had to pay a giant sum to ex-wife number two, and his other expenses were big and immediate. Dukey K. Williams lived like a real Duke would have liked to.

So anyway he owed the money to some big boys in Vegas. They knew he was good for it. Lots of stars lost at the tables before their salaries even hit their pockets. There was nothing unusual about that. The situation was cool.

It was no secret when he started to go with Margaret Lawrence Brown. In her own way she was as famous as he was.

The newspapers and magazines started discussing their relationship as if they were two slabs of prime steak, not human beings with thoughts and feelings.

Then Margaret got a kick about saving the hookers. It wasn't enough she had every little housewife in 'redneck', New Jersey, up in arms and ready for a revolution. No. She wanted the whores. And when Margaret wanted, Margaret got.

Her campaign was slow and clever, and at first people laughed. Save the hookers! For what?

Dukey was also sceptical. Margaret and he had a beautiful sex scene going. He really admired her. But even he didn't believe she was *that* powerful.

But that powerful she was. And suddenly people were not laughing any more, and suddenly Dukey got a few calls, and suddenly, there he was, right in the fuckin' middle.

'Stop your girlfriend's action and we'll forget about your little debt,' was the way the calls started.

And they got heavier and heavier and Dukey tried, he really tried to persuade Margaret to stop, but she didn't want to know.

Eventually Dukey paid the two hundred thousand just to get them off his back. He had to borrow the money from a friend out of his past, a narcotics boss named Bosco Sam. Immediately the threatening calls stopped. A week later Margaret was shot.

Dukey wanted revenge. He wanted it just as much as Rio and Cass and the two sisters he had known nothing about until Margaret's murder.

Their plan was not going to work. Their plan was to grab Enzio Bassalino's three sons by the balls sexually and mentally, destroying their lives, and by so doing reduce the old man to a wreck.

Bullshit.

No chance.

Still, Dukey decided he would let them play around until he was ready to put his own plan into action.

Things were getting involved, but he knew it was going to be *his* way in the end.

Chapter 8

Tall and good-looking, Nick Bassalino was the prodigal Italian–American boy. Fine white teeth, often exposed in a ready smile, warm brown eyes and black hair, slightly curling. He was thirty-three and wore black Italian suits, silk shirts, handmade shoes. Nothing but the best for Nick Bassalino.

He lived in style in a large house high above the lights of Hollywood. Not an actor, he had had many offers because of his almost unbelievable good looks. It was only on close scrutiny that you would suspect his nose was fixed, his teeth capped, his jet-black hair ever so slightly helped along by a bottle of dye.

Nick was head of a company called Warehousing Incorporated. An all-encompassing business, it dealt in every aspect of car stealing, truck stealing, hiding out. It was the biggest outfit of its kind on the West Coast and Nick was in charge.

When your father was Enzio Bassalino you certainly didn't start at the bottom.

Nick's current ladyfriend was April Crawford, an ageing movie star with four husbands behind her. The starlets and the ding-a-lings were not for Nick. He liked to command a little respect when he went out, and in Hollywood the surest way of doing that was to be seen with a movie star.

They had been together a year, and the arrangement suited both of their public images.

April was pleased by the fact that Nick had his own money and didn't sponge off her. He looked good, wasn't too young—not a baby— nothing to make a laughing stock of her. He got along with all her friends—male and female. And of course—most important as far as April was concerned—he was great in bed.

As for Nick, he enjoyed the respectability of it all. Mixing with the movie colony, pictures in the fan magazines, a little class in his life.

He could not understand why Enzio objected so strongly. Enzio was always phoning him and complaining. 'What's with you and the old bag? What's going on? You're making the name Bassalino a laughing stock.'

'Better I should be with a piece of beautiful,

dumb eighteen-year-old cooze, I suppose,' Nick would reply.

'And why not? What's so terrible about a pair of firm knockers, a pretty face, a piece other men want—but you've got.'

'You just don't know . . .' Nick would say, tired of the same old argument.

'OK, so I don't know. But I haven't done too bad for an old man who doesn't know, and *you* haven't done too bad by being my son.'

'All right, all right. Forget it. I'll send you a greetings wire when we break up.'

'Schmuck!' Enzio would mutter, and they both would laugh.

They had a relationship based on love. The fierce, proud love that binds an Italian family.

Whatever Enzio had done in his life, and he had done a lot, he knew he had always been a good father to his boys. In spite of their mother's ill-health (Enzio always referred to Rose's madness as ill-health), he had brought them up to be fine men. Nick was doing a good job of running Warehousing Incorporated. He was tough all right, people thought twice about messing with him. He was a true son of Enzio Bassalino.

* * *

'Are you ready yet, darling?' April Crawford approached Nick in his dressing-room.

They had separate houses, but on weekends April liked Nick to stay with her.

She was a well-preserved blonde in her early fifties. Petite, slim, perfectly groomed and made up. From a distance she looked late thirties, but close up, little tired lines and faint puffiness gave her secrets away.

'I'm always ready for you, sugar,' Nick said, grabbing her, making her squeal with delight.

He had been eight years old when he had seen her on the screen for the first time and had fallen in love with her.

'I think we should be early tonight,' April said. After four husbands and numerous lovers she had never experienced such delights as Nick had to offer.

'You're the boss.'

'I wish we didn't have to go at all. Perhaps if I phoned Janine she would understand . . .'

'She would not understand,' Nick said firmly. 'Besides which, we're both dressed and you look great—like a little doll.' He did not want to miss Janine Jameson's party. She was a contemporary of April's, and equally famous.

They rode to the party in Nick's black Mercedes. April was wearing a pale blue sequin dress, and some of the sequins had come off and stuck to Nick's clothes. He picked them off impatiently.

'Don't lean on me with that dress,' he warned. He always liked to look immaculate.

'You're so fussy,' April laughed, 'but I love you all the same.'

At the party there were many familiar faces, a lot of stars. Nick basked in the company.

A busty starlet approached him at the bar as he was getting April a drink. They had balled once, before he met April.

'How's it going, Nicky Ticky?' the girl asked, thrusting her well-developed mammaries close against him. 'Getting fed up with the old bag yet? 'Cos you know any time you do, I'll be glad to hear from you.'

'What are you going to do when your tits drop?' Nick asked coldly. 'Better stop hustling and take yourself a typing course because it doesn't look to me like it's going to be too long.'

'Cocksucker!' the girl muttered, furious.

'Excuse me, I have a *lady* waiting,' Nick said amiably.

April didn't drink well. After four Scotches her speech started to slur, and shortly after that her walk became lopsided and her face went slack. In short, she fell to pieces.

It irritated Nick. He didn't drink much himself, in his business it paid to be alert, so he usually stuck to plain tonic water. He was always warning April to cut her intake. He tried to mix her drinks himself, carefully watering them down. But she was on to him and grabbed a fresh drink from every passing waiter.

Janine Jameson's party was no exception and April was soon well gone.

Nick knew by experience to keep away from her for a while. Drunk, April became belligerent and insulting.

He was talking to a lady gossip-writer when he first saw the girl. She was standing by the bar with a group of people. She was of medium height with olive, suntanned skin, and a mane of auburn streaked hair. She had an exquisite body, clad in a clinging white dress, long, slit almost to the waist. She was about the most beautiful girl Nick had ever seen—and in his time Nick had seen a lot of girls.

'Who is *that*?' Nick asked.

The lady gossip-writer smiled. A crisp, bitchy, smile. 'Better not let April hear the hard-on in your voice. That's Lara Crichton, one of those poor little rich girls always in the fashion magazines.'

Nick changed the subject.

Lara had spotted him immediately. After all she had pictures of him, a short dossier of his life, she knew all about his relationship with April Crawford.

She observed him across the room and then angled herself at the bar so that when he glanced up she was right in his line of vision. She saw him look, the double-take, the asking who she was.

First part easy—but then the initial impact had always been easy for Lara.

Ever since she could remember men had noticed her. Even when she was a little girl of six and been sent to London she had attracted much attention.

Very pretty, she had had no trouble twisting the childless couple she was sent to round her little finger.

They worshipped her, and although they didn't have much money they lavished all they did have on her.

She became used to attention, and as she developed and grew up she certainly received it.

At fourteen she left school to study dancing, diction and movement. She entered a charm competition in a magazine and won. The prize was a trip to Hollywood. The one good thing about the trip was being able to spend time with Margaret.

On her return to London she found more and more modelling work. She started out as a house model and soon progressed to photographic work. She had a chameleon quality, an essential for a good model. She could look girlish, sophisticated, sexy, even plain. It was a matter of expression, and Lara mastered the art.

She concentrated on her work above all else. She didn't go out on dates. She dieted, exercised, ate health foods and slept at least eight hours every night.

Her incredible beauty deepened and bloomed. She added polish to the diamond.

She started to go out with specially selected men. One could teach her about wine, one about racing, and another about baccarat, *chemin de fer.*

She refused to sleep with them. She hadn't found the man yet to teach her about sex.

When she was twenty she met Michael Crichton, and she knew at once that this was the man she had to marry. Michael had already inherited a trust fund worth over a million, and there was plenty more to come. He was young, good-looking and spoilt. He was also surrounded by girls, and although his initial reaction to Lara was predictable, she knew that if she wasn't very careful she could sink without a trace into the sea of females around him.

So she played it very smart. She refused to go out with him at all. Instead she cultivated his friends so that everywhere he went she was bound to be.

His very best friend, Eddie Stephen Keyes, fell in love with her and proposed. However, she wasn't prepared to settle for anything less than her original prospect.

It took several months for her to get through to Michael. And then suddenly one day he knew, and that was that. They chartered a jet, and got married in Tahiti, and the world press embraced them as the latest Beautiful Couple.

The marriage lasted exactly a year. A year during which Lara became a celebrity.

Then suddenly it was over, they both wanted

a divorce. They were both bored by the restrictions of marriage, the drudgery of being with each other all the time. They were quite friendly about it. Michael agreed to pay her a generous settlement, and she went to Mexico and got a quick divorce, and then on to Acapulco where she met her first Italian Prince. And since that time Lara had moved around. All the best places at the best times with the best men.

It was only when Margaret was shot that Lara had stopped to think. What was she doing with her life? Why was it so important to her to be in the right place at the right time with the right man? Why did she constantly seek out hedonistic men? Why was it so important to be photographed at every airport, quoted in every empty fashion magazine? Why did she need to travel down the Nile, go to Africa, just to be photographed in the newest clothes?

On reflection it all seemed so empty, such a nebulous life. The death of Margaret, the travelling to New York and spending time with Margaret's friends, had somehow made her realise this.

She was determined to help, her mind had been made up to do something. The revenge had been the perfect opportunity.

It had been Rio's idea. They couldn't kill, they weren't murderers, and anyway the man who had pulled the trigger on Margaret had been dispatched by Lola with a bullet straight through the balls. Poetic justice, Rio had enthused, Margaret would have enjoyed that.

They had hired detectives to get a background on Enzio Bassalino, and the one indisputable fact that shone out through his life was that the only things he cared about were his sons, Frank, Nick and Angelo.

If one wanted to hurt Enzio Bassalino, there were three logical ways to go about it.

Lara had been brought to the party by Susie and Les Larson, a young couple whose only claim to fame was that Les's mother was one of the richest women in the world. Lara had arrived the night before. She was their houseguest. Within a week she knew she would have met Nick Bassalino, as April Crawford was an avid partygoer, but to see him so soon was pure luck.

She mentioned him to Susie to gauge her reaction. 'Who is that man?'

'Oh, Nick,' Susie replied with a laugh, 'he's April Crawford's boyfriend. He's strictly not up for grabs, he seems absolutely mad about her, follows her around like a nanny. Why? Do you think he's attractive?'

'Is he an actor?' Lara asked, countering the question.

'No, he's some sort of hustler, wheeler dealer. Les says he's a gangster.' Susie giggled, 'You *do* find him attractive.'

'Not really,' Lara yawned, 'a bit too obvious. All tight trousers and teeth.'

'Yes,' Susie nodded, 'anyway as I said he's well taken care of, and hardly your style.'

Lara wondered exactly what Susie thought her style was.

The party was a bore, and Lara was tired. Sammy Albert, an actor with the reputation of super stud, was trying to persuade her to split and go to the Discothèque with him. She had told him no five times, but he was enamoured and followed her around trying to get her to change her mind.

She told him she wanted to meet April Crawford, and he took her over and introduced her. April's eyes were bloodshot and her lipstick smeared.

Lara smiled and flattered her, and they discussed a mutual friend in Rome, then Nick appeared, and deftly removed the too-full glass from April's hand, which was slopping down her dress, and replaced it with a half-full one.

'Do you know Nick Bassalino?' April asked, patting him fondly. 'This is Lara—Lara . . .'

'Crichton,' Lara said, looking straight at him and accepting his firm handshake with an equally warm pressure of her own.

He had brown eyes, very friendly, very open.

'Why don't we go to the Discothèque?' Sammy asked yet again. 'Nick? April? Maybe you can persuade Lara to come.'

'Oh, lovely idea,' April said. 'I feel like dancing, and Janine's parties—dear girl that she is—do get rather stuffy.'

'Will you come?' Sammy asked Lara.

She nodded, 'I'll just check with Les and Susie.'

'How about that?' Sammy said as she walked away. 'Really something!'

April laughed, 'Sammy darling, every time you meet a new girl it's always a grand love affair for about a week.'

'Just give me a week with this one and I'll be happy.'

Lara returned then, and they left. She travelled with Sammy in his Maserati, while April and Nick followed in the Mercedes.

'I could easily lose them,' Sammy said. 'We could go by my place and pick up some outasite grass. What do you say?'

'I gave it up,' Lara said.

'Oh!' Sammy was speechless. He received thousands of fan letters a week from girls merely wanting to touch him, and this one didn't even want to go with him to his house. It had been a long time between turndowns.

The Discothèque was crowded as usual, but a table was soon cleared for Sammy Albert and April Crawford. Movie stars always got premium treatment, it was one of the fringe benefits.

April ordered a double Scotch, and immediately dragged Sammy off on the tightly packed dance floor.

'They're old friends,' Nick remarked, 'Sammy got his first part in one of April's films.'

'That's all right,' Lara smiled, 'I don't mind, do you?'

'Hell, no, I like April to enjoy herself, does her good, she's a great little gal, got a lot of energy, a real tiger!'

Lara looked at him intently to see if he was putting her on, but he didn't appear to be, he was watching April on the dance floor, a proud smile on his face.

'You and Sammy must be about the same age,' Lara remarked.

'I don't know,' Nick shrugged, 'who cares about age. April's got more energy in her little finger than I have in my whole body.'

April this, and April that. Nick Bassalino was not going to be quite as easy to crack as Lara had imagined. She was used to men falling about—married, single, it made no difference. One of Lara's famous quotes that circulated amongst the jet set was 'most men are easy lays'. She had always found that if there was a man she wanted, he was to be had. Not that there had been that many: the Count, he had lasted two years; the film star, only a few short months; the German Prince, a year; the English Lord, eighteen months; the Greek shipowner, nearly a year; and then Prince Alfa Masserini. She had thought that perhaps he was the right one. He had the film star's looks, the Greek shipowner's money, the English Lord's youth, and the Count's charm. But in spite of it all he had turned out to be a self-centered egoist. Like me, Lara thought, with a short brittle laugh.

'What are you laughing at?' Nick enquired.

'Nothing that would amuse you,' she shook her head in a languid, sexual fashion, so that her long, thick hair swirled forward.

He glanced at her quickly. She was incredibly beautiful. But what was beauty in a town like Hollywood? So many girls, so many different shades of sexy, pretty and beautiful. So many different shapes and sizes. Something to appeal to everyone. In Hollywood beauty was a commodity, a close relation of the hard sell.

April was something else. April was class, and distinction, and acceptance. April was a ticket to ride up there amongst all the movie idols that Nick had worshipped since he was a little kid.

Oh no, he wasn't going to blow April out for a quick dip in the honey pot. She was a jealous lady, and sharp, and full of pride. And if she ever caught him the shit would certainly hit the fan in no uncertain fashion.

'I hope you're coming to the party Susie and Les are giving for me tomorrow night,' Lara said.

'April makes all our arrangements, but I'm sure she knows about it, and knowing my April she never misses a party.'

Lara smiled and widened her eyes. 'Great', she murmured. What a schmuck this guy was—what a dense, stupid schmuck.

Chapter 9

Frank Bassalino was Enzio's eldest son and because of that fact it was he on whom Enzio most depended.

When Enzio had opted out into semi-retirement, it was to Frank that some of his most important business enterprises had been entrusted.

'One day,' Enzio was proud of saying, 'one day that boy is going to be the Man.'

Frank got along well with Enzio's elder business associates. They were difficult men, quick to criticise, but Frank was holding his own nicely. In some ways he was a stronger man than Enzio, born and brought up in one of the harder districts of New York, he had none of Enzio's inborn Sicilian softness.

Frank was not a man to cross. Thirty-six years old, he had worked for his father since he was sixteen, and he had seen all aspects of Enzio's business life. He had been involved in protection, prostitutes, dope, the numbers racket, hoisting. At one time he had enjoyed being the hit man. But Enzio hadn't liked him doing that, it was too risky and too dangerous.

He had been a womaniser, going through an incredible amount—used and thrown away like so many old Kleenex. Until at the age of twenty-nine he had seen a picture of his cousin in Sicily and he had sent for her. She was fourteen years old and did not speak a word of English. Enzio paid her family a dowry, and arranged everything, then Frank married her.

Now twenty-one, she still didn't speak much English. They lived in an old Brownstone house in Queens with their four children, and she was expecting another.

Frank didn't stray too much. The occasional hooker that he could beat up on was about his only weakness.

Rio wanted the chance at him, but she was out-voted. She wasn't his scene, not his style at all. No, the only chance with Frank Bassalino was someone fresh, a sense of innocence. Someone who would remind him of his wife when he had first brought her to America.

Beth was the obvious choice.

There was the perfect opportunity. Frank was looking for a nanny to teach his children

English. He had registered with three employment agencies, and turned down all the applicants who had mostly been black or Mexican.

Beth applied for the job. She changed her hippy clothes and wore a simple blouse and skirt. Hair tied back, scrubbed face, false references.

A maid showed her into a living-room to wait. It was an old-fashioned room with worn furniture and religious pictures on the wall.

She waited half an hour, and then Frank strode in, his wife hovering behind him.

He was a big powerful man. Black hair, black eyes, a moody mouth, beaky nose. He was attractive in a very strong way.

Beth hated him on sight. She knew men like him, big men who resented any change, whose physical strength was their prime weapon.

She remembered the night at the commune when men like him had come calling in the middle of the night. There had been eight or nine of them, and they were drunk.

They had roared up in two cars, laughing and swigging from bottles of booze. The farm was well off the main road. There were no neighbours, no one whom they could ask for help.

The front door wasn't locked, and the men had come bursting drunkenly in. There was an old sheepdog, Rex, and they had kicked him until he was a beaten pulp. They had dragged the girls out of bed and raped them one by one.

And the boys they had beaten up, laughingly, methodically. They had jeered, and called them names, and told them to get a haircut and a job and stop piss-assing around.

It was no match. The men were big and strong and filled with the righteous power of do-gooders.

'If you were my daughter,' one of the men had hissed at Beth as he pumped away inside her, 'I'd tan your hide until you couldn't walk for a week.'

Before they left they cut the boys' hair—crudely with kitchen scissors they hacked and tore away. Max had needed seventeen stitches in his scalp.

It had happened two years before, yet Beth still slept unsoundly, still felt a feeling of revulsion when faced with a man like Frank.

'Hmm,' Frank stared at her briefly. 'You're a little young, aren't you?'

'I'm twenty,' Beth replied. 'I've been working with children for the last three years. Did you see my references?'

Frank nodded. He was surprised at such a young, pretty girl. It was almost too good to be true after some of the garbage the agency had sent to him. The kids would love this one, she looked so clean and nice.

'Listen, you want the job—it's yours. One hundred a week, good room, food, coupla nights a week off. You want to see the children?'

'Yes—I would like to.'

'Hey—Anna Maria,' he pulled his wife forward, a shy, dark girl with puffy features and a huge belly. 'You take—er—what's your name again?'

'Beth.'

'Yeah, of course. Beth, this is Mrs Bassalino—she don't talk too much English—maybe you teach her some too. She'll take you to see the kids, show you around. Any problems you come to me, but I'm a busy man so like make sure there aren't too many problems. When can you start?'

'Tomorrow.'

'Good girl, Anna Maria's going to pop any time now. A little bit of help is just what we need.'

He smiled at them both, gave Anna Maria a gentle shove in Beth's direction, gave Beth one more quick lookover, and left.

Chapter 10

Angelo Bassalino had been sent to London after the trouble. It was only a temporary move, a discreet way of getting rid of him until the Camparo family calmed down. Gina Camparo was to be married soon, and after the ceremony—a few months perhaps—then the whole incident would be forgotten and Angelo could be brought safely home.

Enzio had been somewhat amused by the whole affair. Angelo was his true son, a boy who let nothing stand in the way of his prick.

But it had been a touchy situation, and if Angelo had not been Enzio's son he might have found himself lodging inside a block of cement at the bottom of the East River. To screw a girl was one thing, but not at her engagement party to another man, and not where her brother and fiancé could discover you. And not when the girl was the daughter of a powerful rival—albeit a friendly one.

So Angelo was dispatched to London. There were gambling interests he could take care of there, and Enzio arranged everything.

Angelo was not up to his expectations businesswise, he had none of the Bassalino drive or ambition, he had no hard core of toughness to use when dealing with people.

Enzio reasoned that the boy was only twenty-four, a baby, he had plenty of time to wise up. But Enzio also remembered himself at twenty-four, a veteran of six successful hits, already Crazy Marco's right-hand man, he had a big future ahead of him.

In New York, Angelo had worked for Frank. 'He's a lazy little punk,' Frank complained, 'you send him to a joint to shake loose some tight cash, and you have to send another guy looking for him because he's shacked up with some broad. Cooze, that's all he's got on his mind.'

Enzio tried sending him out to the Coast to work for Nick, but that was even worse. He fell for a sexy starlet, and ended up getting his ass beaten off by her 'producer'.

'You had better pull yourself together in London,' Enzio warned him, 'a Bassalino should command respect. Fuck all you want, but remember *work* is the important thing—

money. There are good opportunities for setting up over there, I want you to control our end of it eventually. To start, you work with the Stevesto organisation—they'll show you around.'

Angelo had shrugged. He didn't care much about making money—as long as there was plenty in the family why did he have to work his ass off making more. It didn't make sense. Let Frank and Nick keep the Bassalino respect going—they enjoyed it, he didn't.

However, he didn't argue with his father. Nobody argued with Enzio. There had been a time when he had expressed a wish not to go into the family 'business'. He wanted to be an actor, or maybe a musician. He had been sixteen at the time. Enzio had beaten him with a leather strap, and locked him into his room for a week—Angelo had not mentioned it again.

London was a fine town, as Angelo soon discovered. Lots of pretty girls, and friendly people, you could walk the streets without the fear of getting beaten up and robbed.

An apartment had been arranged for him, and he went to work for the Stevesto set-up. It was easy potatoes, just keeping his eye on a couple of casinos, and getting the hang of things.

Angelo was happy. A different girl every week if he felt like it, and he did feel like it. He had to have sex every day, it was a habit—like morning coffee or doing push-ups—a habit which he enjoyed excelling at.

Angelo was not big and tall like his two brothers, and was more slight in build, almost skinny. His face was more angular, boned, and his hair was thick and long—a minor freakout. He featured a Ché moustache and beard.

'You look like a fucking communist,' Enzio was always screaming at him. 'Why don't you cut off that hair, get some decent clothes—a suit—look clean, decent, like your brothers.'

Angelo kept his personal appearance as he wanted. It was about the only way he could spit in his father's eye.

The full contingent of English press turned out at Heathrow Airport to meet Rio Java. Undisputed Queen of the Underground Movies, notorious public personality, fashion freak, mother of four children of various colours. Her reputation always preceded her.

She was over six feet tall, thin to almost skeleton proportions, a long, dramatic face, emphasised by the fact that she had shaved off her eyebrows, and wore very sweeping purple false lashes—top and bottom. She was part Cherokee Indian, and part Louisiana hillbilly.

A heroin addict at eighteen, she had been discovered in a hospital by Billy Express who was making a film about drugs called *Turn On*. She had become a star, his camera watching her every move as she was given the treatment—the cure.

Instant stardom. She had his baby (filmed of course). He was very rich, the more pornographic of his movies had made a fortune.

He moved her in with him and his entourage in an elegant New York house he shared with his mother.

She was grateful to him for helping her get off the heroin and she joined him on his constant LSD trips.

There was a Chinese boy, Lei, who shared Billy's bed whenever Rio didn't. It amused Billy to have them make it together for the first time on film.

The result was Rio became pregnant again, and Billy was delighted. He loved children. He had the top floor of the house redecorated as a nursery, and Rio had twins—two tiny Chinese boys.

They were all happy. Billy, his quiet little mother, Lei, the children, the entourage. They made their movies, and threw outrageous parties and existed in a sort of delicious, stoned vacuum.

One day Rio met Larry Bolding. He was a very straight married senator in his middle forties. He came to one of Billy's parties, and Rio took one look at the sun-tanned face, the suit, the honest eyes and she flipped right out.

'I *have* to have him,' she whispered to Billy.

'Easy,' Billy replied, 'pop this in his drink, no problem.'

In a rare moment of clarity Rio decided against spiking his drink, she wanted him without having to do that. She wanted him to want her.

He was nice, he had a lovely laugh. It took some time to get him to a bedroom. More time to get him undressed. He was so sweet! Wore patterned jockey shorts and an undershirt.

Rio launched into her specialties. He was more interested in straight screwing.

It was the start of a three-month affair. An affair which had to be kept secret, due to the fact that he was married and all. Rio understood. He gave her the bullshit about how he and his wife just stayed together for appearances, and worldly as Rio was, she believed him. She told Billy she couldn't sleep with him any more. In fact, because Larry didn't like her whole set-up, she moved out, and took an apartment in the Village. It was more convenient for Larry, more private. Billy gave her money, he kept the children and she went to visit them every day. He wanted her to do another movie, after all she was his superstar.

Larry didn't want her to work, he wanted her always available as he never knew when he could make it to see her.

Rio was in love. She turned very straight for Larry, doing everything he wanted; no drugs, no drinking, no parties, no screwing (except for him), no make-up, no weird clothes.

His visits grew fewer and fewer. Eventually they stopped altogether.

Rio was destroyed. She tried to contact him, but the barriers were up. There was no way of getting past the many secretaries and aides, no way of letting him know she was pregnant with his child.

She slashed her wrists and fortunately was found by a neighbour. The neighbour was Margaret Lawrence Brown.

It took Rio a long time to get over the way Larry Bolding had treated her. She developed a deep resentment for the way women were used by men. She listened to Margaret, and her words made sense. She got herself together, had the new baby. Billy Express wanted her to come back to the house, but she realised that wasn't the way she wanted to live any more. She wanted her children to come and live with her. Billy said no, they would stay with him. There was a long-drawn-out court battle, and she won. She got her children in spite of the abuse Billy publicly hurled at her.

They all got up in the witness box and testified about what a bad mother she was, all her so-called friends.

Margaret Lawrence Brown testified on her behalf, and she got her children.

It was one of the biggest court cases of the year as far as publicity was concerned.

Afterwards, Rio was inundated with film scripts. Everyone wanted to use her. She started to work again and never looked back.

Now she was in London and she was there for a purpose.

Angelo Bassalino.

Chapter 11

Old friends though they were, Bosco Sam wanted his money back, with interest, and Dukey K. Williams just did not have it.

Dukey was hanging around in New York, still living in the apartment he had shared with Margaret.

'Come on, man, we gotta get back in action,' his manager pleaded daily.

'Cancel everything,' Dukey told him, 'I just want to sit still a while, and get my head straight.'

So all dates, a European tour, and a major recording session were cancelled.

Several promoters threatened law suits.

Dukey was not making any money, and the money that was coming in from record sales was going all into the pocket of ex-wife number one, and two 'ex-children'. He called them ex-children because his wife had obtained a court order forbidding him to see them.

Dukey called Bosco Sam up. 'I got a deal for you,' he told him.

'I want my money,' Bosco Sam replied mildly. 'If it was anyone but you, Dukey . . .'

They had struggled through school together.

'Let's meet,' Dukey suggested, 'you'll like the deal.'

'OK, OK, I guess us niggers gotta stick together.'

They met at the zoo. Bosco Sam had a thing about privacy, and all his most important contacts were made in public places.

'I'll probably get mobbed,' Dukey complained. But it was a crisp October morning, and the Central Park zoo was almost deserted. They were hardly an inconspicuous pair.

Dukey in his calf-length, belted mink trench coat, boots, and huge shades.

And Bosco Sam, a camel-hair-coated eighteen stone in weight.

'Fuckin' park,' Bosco Sam said, 'only place a deal can get it on any more.'

'Here's the action,' Dukey said, as they strolled in front of the monkeys. 'Word's all around you're about ready to dance with the Crowns. You and them make sweet soul sounds while Frank Bassalino gets the short ones plucked. Beautiful. No sweat. But how would it grab you if I did the plucking? Frank, the brothers, Enzio. The whole Bassalino bag of bones.'

'You?' said Bosco Sam, and he started to laugh.

'Shit, man! You sound like an elephant farting!'

Bosco Sam heaved with even more laughter.

'Listen,' said Dukey, 'I ain't layin' no shit on you, you hear? I'm serious. For the two hundred thou—you're not involved. You and all that are yours got clean hands, you dig it? Ain't no honky pig gonna come knocking on your door. The way will be all clear for you to walk right on in. Ain't nobody gonna know 'bout our little deal 'cept you an' me.'

'Yeah,' said Bosco Sam slowly, 'yeah . . .'

'It'll all be cool. Keep up the pressure until it all just blows . . . And you with a powdered ass ain't nobody can suspect.'

Bosco Sam started to laugh, 'You still cut it. Big fuckin' star, but you still foxy as Puerto Rican tail!'

'I'll throw in a song or two at your daughter's wedding.'

'She's only ten.'

'I'll be around. Hey, baby, how about it? We all set to jive?'

'Yeah, I'll give you a shot at it. Results or no deal. Who you gonna use?'

'I got a couple of ideas.'

Bosco Sam spat on the ground, 'Use Leroy

Jesus Bauls. He'll cost you, but that black motha don't know no fear, that's why we all call him Black Balls!"

One of the monkeys let out a loud screech.

'Shit!' exclaimed Dukey, 'that monkey just pissed all over me!'

THE LOVE KILLERS

teen looks. He'll cool us, but that black
music don't know no man, that's why we sitting here black Bella."

"One of the Journeys is one a tough street."

She confirmed Dewey. What money had
pissed all over that.

Chapter 12

Lara's effect on Nick was slow but lethal.

They met again at the party Susie and Les threw for her, and then again at a screening of the new Warren Beatty film.

Lara was seeing Sammy Albert, fighting him off because to get involved sexually with anyone was a diversion she did not need. It was at her suggestion that Sammy invited April and Nick to dinner at the Bistro.

Confident that this was the night, Sammy was in a buoyant mood. Lara wore her Yves Saint Laurent black velvet jacket, cut man's style, and underneath a high-necked shirt in black chiffon which, when you looked closely, was see-through. She wore no bra, and the effect was incredibly sexy because as she moved, the jacket moved, exposing her, and then falling back into place.

'Now you see them, now you don't,' Sammy announced proudly at the beginning of the evening.

Nick and April started to row half-way through dinner, a whispered row that no one was supposed to notice because above all April would never blow her image by being jealous.

The champagne that Sammy had insisted on was beginning to have its effect. 'Get your eyes off her bloody tits!' April hissed.

Nick, who had been making a concentrated effort *not* to look, was insulted. 'Just cool it, April,' he muttered.

'Cool it,' April mimicked, 'just who do you think you're talking to, little man?'

'I'm talking to you, and you've had enough.' He gripped her wrist as she went to lift her glass. Furious, she tried to shake free, and the champagne spilled and splashed on the sleeve of her dress.

'Oh, dear,' Lara was the first there with a napkin, dabbing it dry, 'I don't think it will stain.'

'It's only an old dress,' April said, recovering her composure and smiling. 'Nick, you're *so* clumsy.' She turned to talk to Sammy on her other side.

Lara glanced at Nick and smiled sympathetically. He smiled back, letting his eyes drop briefly to her breasts. If he was going to get accused of it he may as well do it. She was still looking at him, the smile gone, the eyes probing and interested.

He felt a sudden uncomfortable tightness in his trousers, a feeling he had long ago learned to control. Christ, this girl was really something, she was getting to him in no uncertain way. In the year he had been with April he had only taken chances twice. Once, on a business trip to Vegas, a faceless showgirl with incredible legs. The other, a girl he had met at the beach on one of his rare afternoons off. Neither of the girls had known who he was, or anything about him. That way there was no risk of April ever finding out.

'Let's go to the Discothèque,' Sammy was saying.

'Yes, marvellous idea,' April agreed. She was downing yet another glass of champagne.

Nick didn't try to stop her. Tonight it was her problem, let her get good and boozed up. She would be sorry in the morning.

There was more champagne at the Discothèque, and Lara noticed that even Nick was drinking, something she had never seen him do before.

She danced with Sammy, and was embarrassed by his convulsive almost obscene way of moving. One thing about European men, they knew how to keep their cool when dancing. Sammy hopped about like a baby elephant jerking off.

When she sat down April invited her to the Ladies' Room. She went because half the initial battle was remaining friendly with April.

'I think you're right, darling,' April observed. 'Look at my dress, all dry and not a stain in sight. Do you have a comb?'

They stood side by side, observing themselves in the wall-length mirror. April could easily have been Lara's mother, but she didn't realise this. As far as she was concerned her reflection was just as smooth and youthful as the girl beside her.

'Isn't Sammy a darling boy?' she said, 'such fun. I hope you realise how lucky you are.'

'Lucky?' Lara questioned.

'Well, of course, darling, he's *very* much in demand, and I can see that he's absolutely mad about you.'

Lara smiled slightly, she sensed what was coming next.

'Real men are few and far between in this town,' April hiccoughed elegantly. 'I should know, I married four of them. Now take Nick, for instance, a good-looking man, but what does he have to offer, darling? There's more to it than just being a good fuck. Confidentially I need a little more from a man, you know what I mean?'

Lara nodded. 'Yes, I know what you mean.' What April meant was—stick with Sammy and keep your hands off Nick.

April examined her teeth closely in the mirror. 'I do like your blouse, darling, you must tell me where you got it. Of course Nick's not a man for boobs, he's a leg man.' April hoisted her skirt and exposed still perfect legs. 'Also I doubt very much if he'd allow me to wear a top like that. He's really very prudish, it's the Italian side of him, you know. Ah well, back to the champagne.'

Lara lingered in the Ladies' Room. April didn't have to tell *her* about Italians, the only time they were prudish was if you were their wife. She wondered if Nick wanted to marry April, she was still a good-looking woman for her age, and of course there was the fame thing. April Crawford was a name that had been right up there with Lana Turner, Ava Gardner, and the other famous Crawford. Lara knew a lot about Nick, but there was still plenty to find out.

She went back inside, and April was dancing with Sammy.

She took off her jacket, and Nick glanced quickly at her. 'You want to dance?' he asked.

She nodded. They got up and he took her by the arm and steered her to the small, tightly packed dance floor. Curtis Mayfield was at full shout.

They faced each other and went through the ritualistic moves. He was a good dancer, tight, controlled and at ease. The sounds were too loud to talk. Then suddenly the music changed and Isaac Hayes was singing 'Never Can Say

Goodbye', and it was slow, throbbing and sensual.

Nick was staring at her, his brown eyes very moody. He pulled her slowly towards him, his nails digging into her bare flesh under the black chiffon. Lara stared back, and when she was close to him she felt the proof of his attraction for her and for one short moment the music, the feel of his maleness, it all combined to make her want to forget everything, and just be with this man.

She surrendered to the feeling, and pressed close against him.

'Hey, baby, I don't have to tell you how I feel,' he muttered, 'no—I don't have to tell you—you know—you knew from the first time we saw each other.'

She managed to push him away a little and shake her head slowly.

'I've got to see you,' Nick was saying. 'What about lunch tomorrow? We could meet somewhere at the beach, somewhere quiet where no one would see us.'

'Wait a minute,' Lara pushed him away completely and they stood in the midst of the swaying dancers, '*I* can see you any time, *I'm* not tied down.'

Nick pulled her back to him. 'Listen, baby, you know my scene with April. She's a lovely little lady, and I wouldn't want to do anything to hurt her.'

'Then don't,' Lara said crisply, back in control.

'Ah, come on,' Nick said, 'you feel the same way I do, I *know* you do. If I was to slide my hand under those tight pants of yours I could prove it to you—you'd be ...'

She cut him short, her eyes suddenly wide, appealing. 'I'm not arguing. Let's go home now. You say goodbye to April and I'll kiss Sammy on the cheek. I'll take off my tight pants for you and ...'

'Hey, you're a bitch.' He was angry.

Her green eyes gleamed. 'I'm not a bitch, I'm just honest. If we both want each other so much, what's the hang-up?'

'You *know* the hang-up,' he groaned.

'Yes, I do, and it's all yours.' Lara walked off the dance floor and rejoined the others. She was pleased with the way things were going. It was a beginning.

Chapter 13

The only day that Beth saw Frank Bassalino was Sunday. It appeared to be the only day he was home. Weekdays he was up and away before anyone was awake, returning late in the evenings after the household was asleep.

Sunday was his day with the children. In the morning he would take them to the park, then home for a huge lunch of various pastas that Anna Maria would spend the morning preparing. In the afternoon he would play with them, absorbing himself in their interests. Cars and trains with the two boys, perhaps a game with the six-year-old girl—his obvious favourite—and complicated building games with the two-year-old.

He was a good father, if you could call devoting one day a week to his children being a good father.

Anna Maria was a placid, almost stupid girl. She had no particular desire to learn English. Frank and the children conversed with her in Italian, and since Frank and the children were her whole life, what was the point? She spent her days baking and sewing and writing letters to her family in Sicily. She rarely left the house.

Beth found the job extremely boring. The children were well behaved and easy to manage. She gave them an hour's coaching in English a day, and they seemed to enjoy it, even the little ones. There wasn't much else to do. The older children went to school, and the two-year-old slept in the afternoons.

After two weeks she met with Cass. 'I don't think it's going to work,' she said, 'I never get to see him.'

Cass nodded. 'Listen, it's a crazy idea anyway. I don't think you should be involved any more.'

Beth thought of the commune, of her own child and her friends. It was a tempting thought to agree with Cass, pack her things and leave. But that would be admitting defeat, and Beth wanted to accomplish just as much as the others.

'What about Lara and Rio? How are they making out?' she asked.

'All seems to be going well,' Cass replied. 'I'm

going to meet with Dukey tonight. I'm sure he agrees with me about you. You shouldn't be involved.'

'Why not?' Beth's face started to flush, 'I'm Margaret's sister. *I* want to do something just as much as the others.'

'Beth, you just aren't cut out to be involved. I said so from the beginning.'

'Well, I am involved now, and I don't want to stop.'

That evening Beth waited. She put on a long white cotton nightdress, frilled and virginal. She brushed her straight blonde hair out loose. She looked very young and pretty.

Her room overlooked the front of the house, and at two a.m. a car drew up with three men inside it. Two got out and went to the front door, and then one returned to the car and it drove off. Frank was safely home.

She remained at the window, her mouth dry with fear. She knew Frank's routine. He went to his dressing-room where he changed, and then into the big, old-fashioned kitchen where he made coffee and toast.

Another car moved slowly past the house, its headlights dipped, two men inside. Frank seemed to have bodyguards to look after the bodyguards.

Still she waited, not moving, shivering slightly. What if she went to the kitchen and he wanted her? What then? She didn't know how to manoeuvre people, pull the strings. She wasn't Lara or Rio. Frank Bassalino was a hard, strong man. How did one destroy a man like that?

She thought of Margaret, she thought of the man who had ordered her to be shot. She had decided in her own mind what was to be done.

Frank was brooding and thoughtful. There was trouble all over. The cops were tightening up, more money or more harassment. The Crown gang were causing disturbance, something would have to be done about that. Enzio was driving him mad, phoning him to complain about this and that. He must have spies everywhere. The old fool was supposed to be retired, why didn't he keep his nose out now?

There was also the protection problem. Several restaurants and clubs under the 'security' of Frank Bassalino were being leaned on to put their faith in other directions.

There had been a few unfortunate accidents, and the owners of certain establishments were beginning to wonder why they should pay protection to Frank Bassalino, *and* the police, and *still* get hit.

Frank suspected a black organisation run by narcotics' king Bosco Sam was behind it.

Rumour had it that Bosco Sam had big plans for muscling in on the Bassalino and Crown operations.

Frank had sent out the word that he was

prepared to meet with Bosco Sam, to discuss things.

In the meantime the clubs and restaurants were persuaded it was in their best interests to keep up their payments. It was a problem Frank was confident he could deal with on his own.

Then at home there was Anna Maria with her belly so swollen a man couldn't even get a good fuck any more, and he didn't like to go elsewhere. The last time had been bad. Esther's place, a new girl. Esther *knew* what he was like, so he figured the girl would be prepared. A black-eyed girl, full breasted, and meaty thighed. He had turned her over and rammed it in from behind. A slow count of ten, then wham. He had pulled her head back and had started to slap her, squeezing her breasts, slapping her buttocks.

As he got rougher she started to fight back and he liked that. Then she started to scream, and her nose was bleeding and the whole thing was a mess. The girl was screaming for the police, and it took Esther some time to calm her down.

Frank left, angry, moody. It hadn't been satisfactory. That had been two weeks previous and now he would have to make do with Anna Maria.

Ah, at the beginning she had been so sweet. So ripe and lovely. Young, untouched, innocent. It was at that point in his thoughts that Beth came into the kitchen.

'Excuse me,' she said, 'I didn't realise anyone was up. I couldn't sleep and thought I would make some warm milk.'

'Warm milk is for old maids,' Frank said slowly. He had never realised how pretty she was.

She laughed nervously, and took the milk from the fridge.

He watched her as she bent to take a saucepan from the cupboard and poured the milk in. She wore no make-up, he hated make-up on women. It always reminded him of tarts. Hot, dirty tarts in black bras and suspender belts. The kind his father liked. The kind his father had introduced him to when he was thirteen years of age.

'The job OK?' Frank enquired.

'Yes, thank you, Mr Bassalino.' She concentrated on stirring the milk, a curtain of fine blonde hair falling across her face.

'Kids treat you OK?'

'Yes, they're lovely children,' she turned to look at him, and he liked her clean, scrubbed skin.

She knew then that everything was set. If only she could go through with it and hide her revulsion.

'You're a nice-looking girl,' Frank said, 'how come you want to hide yourself away watching kids?'

'I like to lead a quiet life.'

The milk was starting to boil, and she watched it bubble and froth to the top of the pan and finally cascade over the top and on to her hand.

She screamed with genuine pain and Frank started to say, 'What the f . . .' but then he saw what she had done and he smothered her hand in great globs of butter.

'I'm sorry,' she stared at him with very blue, vulnerable eyes. 'I guess I wasn't concentrating on what I was doing.'

They were close, so close that the very smell of him made her want to run. But instead she leaned closer, and with no warning he picked her up under the arms the way you lift a child, and he started to kiss her—slowly at first, and then stronger, harder.

She didn't say anything, she let her lips stay dry, closed, puckering them slightly.

'Christ!' he said. 'You're so light, like one of the kids. And you don't even know how to kiss. How old *are* you?'

She felt captive in his arms, he had such enormous strength she felt he could crush her if he wanted to.

'I'm twenty,' she whispered.

'Have you ever had a man?'

'Mr Bassalino—please—you're hurting me. Please let go of me.'

He released her abruptly. 'You know what I want to do?' he enquired thickly.

She nodded, lowering her eyes quickly.

'We'll go to your room—no one will know. Have you ever done it before?'

He was hoping she would say no. He hadn't had a virgin since Anna Maria. In fact, the only other women he had been with had all been hookers.

'I'm not a virgin,' Beth said, the rehearsed lines coming easily. 'Once before, I was very young—only twelve. My stepfather, he was drunk. I didn't understand what he was doing. I had a baby. There has been no one since.'

Frank digested the information silently. It appealed to him. One time with a drunken relation, it hardly counted. And only twelve at the time. He slid his hand beneath the bodice of her nightgown.

'Mr Bassalino, I can't,' her eyes were wide with fear. 'Your wife, the children, it's not right . . .'

'I'll pay you.' He watched her shrewdly. 'One hundred dollars—cash. How about that?'

She shook her head. 'I don't think you understand. I do find you an attractive man, but the circumstances are not right. I am employed by you, and have yours and your wife's trust. If we—well you know—how could I face myself tomorrow?'

Frank was impressed by the girl's honesty. He didn't come across many people who had scruples, it made a refreshing change. However, it still didn't solve the problem of what he had for her. 'How about if I fire you?' he said.

She shook her head. He was fascinated by her soft blonde hair, he wanted to wrap it around his feet—other things. He wanted her very badly.

'What do you want?' he asked. By experience he knew that there was always something people wanted.

'I don't want anything,' she said very quietly. 'I knew when I first saw you that I shouldn't have taken the job. You are the first man that I knew would be different, would understand. You are the first man that I have ever wanted, and yet you are married, so it is impossible.'

He wrapped her up in his big arms again and started to kiss her, his hands roamed over her body. Her struggling was futile, he was even stronger than the man who had raped her . . .

She felt exhausted and almost relieved. It would happen soon, it was what he wanted, and it was what she had planned for.

She hardly noticed him carrying her to her room, he kept on telling her it was going to be all right, everything would be fine. She was glad she had smoked the pot earlier, it had taken the edge off things, made her relax more.

He pulled off her nightgown, locked the door, struggled out of his clothes.

'I'm not going to hurt you,' he mumbled. 'It won't be like before.'

She recoiled from the weight of his body, and

shut her eyes tightly as he pushed her legs apart. And then she felt him, and the tension slipped away and she almost smiled.

Frank Bassalino was endowed with no greater gift than a ten-year-old boy.

Chapter 14

Leroy Jesus Bauls stood very still at the door to the restaurant. His hard cinnamon eyes flicked slowly over the occupants, finally coming to rest on one man at a corner table.

The *maître d'* was heading towards Leroy, his mouth open, ready to say there was no room. It was a smart restaurant, and they didn't encourage blacks, even if they were well dressed and expensive looking, like Leroy.

But before the *maître d'* could reach him, Leroy had placed the parcel he was carrying on the floor, given it a swift kick in the direction of the corner table, and turned and left.

The *maître d'* scratched his head in a puzzled fashion and started towards the parcel.

* * *

On television later that night there was a full report of the accident. *The Magic Garden,* a popular Manhattan restaurant, had been blown apart by a bomb. Fourteen people were dead, twenty-four injured. The police were working on several leads.

'Bullshit,' muttered Leroy Jesus Bauls, standing and switching the television off.

'What you say, honey?' a black girl of startling beauty asked. She was mid-twenties, with curled auburn hair and wide brown eyes.

'Nothing,' Leroy replied, 'nothing that would interest you.'

'Everything about you interests me,' the girl whispered, nuzzling up behind Leroy and stroking his hair.

Impatiently he shook her off. How nice it would be to find a girl that could keep her hands off him.

Leroy was twenty-two. Six-foot-three tall, slimly built but extremely strong. Straight features, perfectly symmetric, inherited from his Swedish mother. Dark brown chocolate skin, inherited from his Jamaican father.

He always dressed impeccably. Suits, vests, silk shirts. Even his socks and undershorts were made of the purest silk.

He favoured black as a colour, in clothes, women, cars, furniture.

His mother had given him the taste for

expensive things. His mother had also turned him off white people for life.

'I wonder if we might go to a movie tonight,' the girl asked, 'the late show. I don't have to work tomorrow so . . .'

'I don't think so, Melanie,' Leroy replied quietly, 'I have to work myself later.'

'What do you do?' Melanie enquired. She had known him for three weeks, slept with him for two, and still knew nothing about him except that he had a nice apartment, plenty of money and was interesting to be with.

'I've told you, don't be nosey,' Leroy said, his voice flat. 'I do things—things that wouldn't interest you—deals, business matters.'

'Oh!' Melanie was silent, then, 'What time do you have to go out?'

'Later.'

'Well, I could stay, keep the bed warm. As I don't have to be up early I could stay all night. Would you like that?'

'Yeah—some other time though.'

Melanie's eyes brimmed with tears, she sensed he was going off her. 'You've got another girl,' she accused, 'you're going out to see another girl.'

Leroy sighed. They were all the same. It amazed him. Why couldn't he find a girl who would keep her cool. He always chose very carefully. No hookers, junkies, or hustlers in any sense. He went out with black models, actresses, singers. Melanie, for instance, had recently been on the cover of *Cosmopolitan*, and the girl before her a runner-up in the Miss Black America competition.

'Don't blow your cool,' Leroy hissed, as Melanie started to cry loudly, 'your lovely eyes gonna get all red and runny, and that I don't like.'

'Shall I stay then?' Melanie questioned tearfully.

Leroy shook his head, 'I told you. Didn't I tell you? I got business to conduct.'

Chapter 15

Rio attracted freaks and fags the way a bitch in heat attracts dogs. They clustered around her in thrilled little groups, clad in outlandish clothes, high on anything that happened to be around, gossipy, bitchy.

Rio didn't mind. She could get it together with anyone as far as having a warm, generous relationship was concerned. She looked for the good in everyone and if she didn't find it she looked again.

Straight men were her only difficulty. Like Larry Bolding, for instance. She found they were all full of such ridiculous hang-ups, such dishonesty and bullshit. It turned her off. She became feline and hard, in their company.

Rio had never been to London before, but

she had friends, anxiously awaiting her arrival: Peaches, the gloriously beautiful blonde model who had once been a man; Perry Hernando, fag Mexican singer who prowled London every so often looking for new talent.

They came to her rented apartment accompanied by others. They brought champagne with them and smoked some incredible pot supplied by a middle-aged American lady in low-cut black. Then in cars and taxis they took Rio triumphantly to *Tramp* the only place to go in London according to Peaches and Hernando.

It was exactly were Rio wanted to go. It was the place where Angelo Bassalino appeared nightly with his lady of the week.

She knew all his movements and habits. At the moment he was currently screwing a thin, blonde, bit-part actress, also a married woman with four children, and a fat, rich husband, and a female blackjack dealer from one of the casinos where he worked.

He liked women. Any shape, size or colour. He was not particular.

Rio had not formed a plan of action. She felt very sure and confident. She knew people, she knew she could get into their heads if she wanted to. It would be easy deciding what to do to destroy Angelo.

She wished she could have dealt with all three of them, Frank, Nick *and* Angelo. It was her plan. She should never have told anyone, she could have done it quietly herself.

Lara and Beth, what did they know about beating someone mentally, reducing someone to a wreck, finding the one chink and pressing, pressing until it gave way.

Bullshit! They knew how to get a guy to screw them and that was it. Not like Margaret, she could have done it. Margaret was a witch, she knew everything.

Rio remembered their first meeting. It had been winter, and so cold that Rio could recall how she had first thought of setting the building on fire. It was an insane thought, but at the time she was ready for any way to do it.

What a way to go! One big glorious blaze. But then she had remembered all the other people living there, and also what use would a goodbye note be for Larry Bolding if that went up in flames too. She wanted the shit to suffer. She wanted to ruin him and his whole stinking political career.

She had made her face up very carefully, an extravaganza of exotic colour. A red Halston dress, long and clinging. After all, she was a superstar and she certainly wasn't going to creep out.

She was high. A little acid to help her on the ultimate trip.

It was three o'clock in the morning, and she put on some incredible sounds—loud. She used the razor that Larry kept there, he didn't like electric ones. She slid the fresh blade out and cut a deep line along the inside of her right wrist, then the other. It didn't hurt, the sudden gushing of blood was beautiful, it matched her dress.

She was laughing. It was the best she had felt for months. No hang-ups, no worries, no anything.

She was still laughing when she passed out, the blood pumping out of her cut wrists on to the pure white carpet.

It was all hazy after that. Margaret's face, very close, very concerned. A feeling of movement, being carried. Voices always muffled and far away. And then the awakening—how many days later? Two, three? And Margaret Lawrence Brown sitting at a table writing. Long black hair propped back from a strong face by tinted glasses.

Rio couldn't move. She was in a strange bed in a strange room and her arms were bandaged up to the elbows.

'Hey,' she managed, and Margaret looked up at her, a direct, green-eyed stare, no make-up, full lips, not a beautiful face, not even pretty, but a face of such enormous warmth and attractiveness that Rio immediately liked her. A strange feeling, because what the hell, she didn't even want to be here.

Margaret smiled slightly and got up. Tall, small-bosomed in a loose T-shirt and Levi's. 'I guess you're going to make it,' she said in a gravelly voice. 'It was touch and go there for a time, but I had a feeling you'd pull through. I'm Margaret, I live next door and I happened to get blasted out of bed by the sounds, so since you're usually so quiet, I came over to investigate. You would have made a gorgeous picture for the newspapers—the red dress and the blood and the white rug. It was almost a shame to save you, but baby, you can't do that sort of thing over a guy!' Margaret shook her head in disbelief. 'Larry Bolding's a prick. I don't even know him, but I can tell you he's a prick. Baby, we do not kill ourselves over pricks.'

Margaret never lost any time in making a point.

Rio stayed with her for two weeks before moving back to her own apartment, and she learned more in those two weeks than she had in a lifetime.

Margaret was that rare exception, a truly selfless person. She wanted nothing out of life except to do good for others. She gave her time, her energy, her life, to any cause that she found worthy. And she had a biting furious anger at the way women were treated as second-class citizens. She wanted to change things and like most people she didn't just sit around talking about it, she went out and did what she could.

In the dim recesses of *Tramp* Rio recognised Angelo Bassalino when he came in. She looked him over with a strong and steady stare. He was with a skinny little blonde.

Rio had no plans to waste any time, she walked over to his table and sat herself down.

'Hey, Angelo,' she said, 'what's all this I hear about you being the best fuck in town?'

Chapter 16

Enzio Bassalino placed three phone calls. In order of importance he spoke to Frank in New York first.

'I'm thinking of coming in,' he stated, 'how's the climate?'

Frank knew that Enzio was not referring to the weather. 'The same,' he replied, his voice guarded. He knew for a fact that the FBI had a tap on his phone.

'Well, I think I'll come in anyway,' Enzio growled, 'the usual hotel, the usual set-up—arrange it.'

'I don't think now's the right time,' Frank tried to keep the irritation out of his voice. Why did his father always have to interfere?

'I want to see the grandchildren,' Enzio was

stubborn, 'and clear up some other matters. You know what I mean?'

'Yeah. I know what you mean.'

Frank knew exactly what he meant. He meant the panic that was going on about the bomb going off at the *Magic Lantern*.

Frank had everything in hand. He was calling some meetings and finding out some facts.

At first he had thought it was Bosco Sam, or maybe the Crowns. But information pointed against them.

Tomassio Vitorelli, Frank's counsellor, had been meeting with an informant at the *Magic Lantern* the night the bomb had exploded...

'OK, so arrange it. I'll be in tomorrow. International, three o'clock. Tell Anna Maria to start cooking.'

Enzio hung up. He knew Frank was annoyed, he knew that his eldest son thought he could handle everything himself. But what was wrong with a little insurance? What was wrong with Enzio Bassalino showing his face in New York?

The Crown gang were trying to move in on several enterprises, they weren't succeeding, but they were causing certain 'problems'. What with that and the Protection Business, Enzio felt he should be there. He was sure that with him in town those problems would cease. Perhaps a personal meeting with Rizzo Crown would fix things, they went back many years together so why not?

Next Enzio telephoned Nick in Los Angeles. 'What's happening?' always his opening question.

Nick gave him a short rundown on the latest activities.

'Fine, fine,' Enzio coughed and spat into an ashtray on his desk, a habit that did not endear him to his staff. 'I'm going to New York tomorrow, it might not be a bad idea for you to fly in for a couple of days.'

'Why?' Nick didn't like leaving the Coast. He didn't like his sun-tan suffering for even one day.

'It might be advisable,' Enzio said. 'I'll let you know.'

'Jesus . . .' Nick muttered.

'What's the matter with you?' Enzio boomed. 'Can't you even leave the old bag for two days? What's she got, a direct line to your balls?'

'If it's necessary I'll be there,' Nick said slowly. Maybe a trip to New York wasn't such a bad idea. Maybe it would be the perfect opportunity to get something together with Lara that April couldn't find out about.

'OK, OK, I'll let you know,' Enzio was impatient to get off the phone.

Nick was a stupid boy, any man was stupid who let a woman tie him up by the balls. Enzio had always prided himself on being very clever about women. A piece was a piece and there was plenty of it about. Use them before they could use you, that had always been his motto. Once they became clingy and demanding, that was the time to boot them out.

Mary Ann August came wriggling into the study. Clad in her customary bikini with puffs of backcombed blonde hair, she stood silently picking off her nail varnish until Enzio said, 'Yeah? What is it?'

'Alio's here,' she said, 'he's out by the pool. He wants a sandwich and the cook's out.'

'So make him a sandwich,' Enzio said, delaying his call to Angelo.

'What kind?' Mary Ann asked blankly.

'I don't know, ask him.' Mary Ann was beginning to jar, sometimes big boobs were just not enough.

'There's cheese I guess,' Mary Ann said thoughtfully, 'or cucumber. Do you think he'd like cucumber?'

'How the hell do I know,' Enzio stormed suddenly, 'get out of here, I want to make a call.'

Mary Ann left quickly.

It would have been nice, Enzio mused, if Rose had not gone mad and shut herself away. An old-style wife was not replaceable. A woman who knew her position in life and kept it. It would have been far more convenient to keep his mistresses in separate apartments, visiting them only when necessary, putting up with their stupid chatter only when he wanted to.

But it was too lonely without anyone. He needed to share his bed. Sometimes he had nightmares, dreams from which he awoke shaking and cold around the heart. At those times he stretched out for human contact, the security of another body nearby. He was frightened for his health. What if his heart should falter and no one was near? He had suffered one attack three years before, but the doctors had said he was fine, better than before, no need to worry. But still ... What did doctors know? Enzio didn't trust them.

It would not be a bad idea, Enzio decided, to replace Mary Ann in New York.

He phoned London and could not get hold of Angelo. He was not at the Casino nor at his home. He was out screwing of course, the boy thought of nothing else. Enzio smiled, at Angelo's age he had been just the same.

At Angelo's age he had had the world by the balls. Prohibition, Chicago, a different kind of world to live in, a world of crazy excitement and thrills.

The Bassalino name had rated alongside Capone, Legs Diamond, O'Banion. Enzio sighed with pleasure when he remembered the early days. It was all so different now, with everything hidden under a cake of legitimacy.

Enzio remembered, Alio had been by his side from the beginning.

Enzio chuckled, and walked out to the pool still laughing. He wondered if Alio would remember the time they tried to bribe the chef of their favourite Italian restaurant to put arsenic in an arch rival's soup. The chef had refused and fled the city, and to this day Enzio missed his incredible meatballs.

Chapter 17

They met on the plane like conspirators. Nick was wary checking the first-class section for friends of his or April's. Only after he had done this and found all was clear, did he condescend to join Lara.

She was dressed all in white and looked very beautiful. He decided the risk was well worth taking.

Lara had blankly refused to meet him in Los Angeles, giving him the ultimatum of her or April. How could he possibly choose? He was going to marry April. Lara had turned up at the wrong time. He wanted a scene with her, but he wasn't prepared to risk his future, and his future was being with April Crawford.

Enzio had suggested the New York trip at

just the right moment. Nick had mentioned to Lara that he was going, and hinted that she should come. Surprisingly she had said yes.

'April mustn't find out,' Nick had told her nervously, and for a change she had agreed with him. 'We'll do it your way,' she said.

Nick thought he had the situation well covered. They arrived at the airport separately, boarded the plane separately, they would disembark separately. Who could possibly find out they were together?

Lara had an apartment in New York, and Nick was going to stay at the hotel with Enzio. He figured New York was a big place, you could get lost in New York. It wasn't a nosey little city like Los Angeles where you couldn't even take a piss without everyone knowing.

He just wanted to be with Lara without the fear of April appearing. One or two days should be long enough to get her out of his system. It was just a sex urge, a sudden lust. Oh sure, she was a beautiful girl, and pretty well connected in her own way, but she wasn't April Crawford. April Crawford was a star.

Frank was very demanding, and after the first night he came immediately to Beth's room whenever he arrived home.

He quieted her objections. He reassured her that Anna Maria would not wake up.

She accepted him in the dark old-fashioned room above the kitchen. She accepted his kisses and embraces, the fumbling way he made love. In spite of the revulsion he produced in her, she felt sorry for him. He stood for everything she loathed, and yet there was a certain loneliness in the man that caught her sympathy. Maybe it was the cruel joke that nature had played on him, it made him very vulnerable. It explained why he needed a girl like her, a girl he thought was not experienced and therefore could make no criticism or comparison.

She lived up to expectations. She was soft, warm, appreciative. At the same time she managed to feign a childlike innocence that seemed to fascinate him.

He bought her little presents. One night a cheap charm bracelet, the next a pound of strawberries which he ate. He was a selfish lover, satisfying himself and forgetting about her. It never took him very long, a ten-minute routine which was always the same. He liked her to be in the bed waiting, he insisted she wear the long white nightdress. He would fondle her breasts for a few minutes, then suck at them until he was ready to mount her, a few thrusts and it was over.

By the end of the week he was already talking of finding an apartment for her.

By the end of the week she had already planned how she would arrange to have his wife find them together.

* * *

Lara called Cass as soon as she arrived at her apartment in New York. 'I'm making progress,' she said. 'April should know about us by the morning paper.'

'Are you sure you're all right?' Cass enquired anxiously.

'Perfect,' Lara assured her.

'Once April finds out he flew here with me— he's out. She's too proud to accept seconds. The funny thing is I haven't slept with him.' She paused. 'How's Beth?'

'I don't know. I spoke to her a week ago, she seemed disturbed. I tried to talk her out of it, but she wouldn't listen. I'm very worried.'

'Yes, she's such a child,' Lara thought anxiously of the sister she hardly knew. 'I think we have to insist that she drops out of the whole thing. After all she does have a child at that commune and I think we have to persuade her that the child needs her more than our crazy scheme.'

'Right,' Cass agreed. 'I'll make contact.'

'What about Rio? Any word?'

'A wire saying SUCCESS ASSURED. The agreement was to get in touch every Wednesday. If I can't get in touch with Beth by tomorrow I shall go to the house, pretend I'm a relative or something.'

'Good,' Lara agreed. 'Enzio Bassalino is in New York. That's the reason I'm here.'

'Oh God, I hope Dukey doesn't find out, he's always muttering about there only being one way.'

'Killing's too good for him, our way is best.' Lara was surprised at her own coldness.

She hung up, went to the bathroom, and brushed her luxuriant mane of hair.

She thought she looked tired, faint circles under her deep green eyes. She was worried about Beth. She was such a little kid, so unworldly, stuck away in a commune all her life, and now stuck in a house with some hood. Well, she would just have to rely on Cass to get her out.

Lara thought about Nick. He was stupid—yes. Unintelligent—yes. Conceited—yes. But the funny thing was she liked him, a pure natural like that had nothing to do with money or position or title. It would make everything a lot easier if she didn't. However, she still had a job to do. And with Beth out of the picture it was more important than ever.

Frank arrived at the hotel with Golli and Segal. They accompanied him everywhere, they were his protection, his insurance. The way things were going in New York there was big trouble everywhere. Only the previous week one of Frank's 'executives' had been gunned down in the middle of Manhattan. He was taking no chances, Golli and Segal were worth the exorbitant money he had to pay them each week.

Enzio had used the hotel many times before and his security arrangements were as usual. The entire third floor was inaccessible except to members of his immediate entourage. Even Frank had to use the complicated passwords, although all of the men Enzio travelled with had known Frank since he was a baby.

Enzio did not believe in new faces. He kept a permanent army of twenty-five men who had been with him many years, and were always at his call. Frank had argued with him many times over this. 'They're old guys, what could they do for you? They can barely carry a gun any more, let alone use it!'

Enzio would laugh in his face. 'These old "guys" as you call them are tougher and smarter than any of the young punks that you have around. I *know* I can't be got to—do you have that security?'

Frank felt safe enough with Golli and Segal, they were young and fast, and he had seen them in action.

Enzio greeted Frank warmly. They kissed and hugged, and murmured words of greeting in Italian.

'So, you look OK,' Enzio announced, 'how's the little girl? She about ready to pop again?' He was very fond of Anna Maria.

Frank nodded. 'She's fine, looking forward to seeing you.' But his thoughts were not of his wife. His thoughts were of Beth.

'The babies? They looking forward to see their grandpop?'

'Yeah, of course, dinner tonight, Anna Maria's making your favourite spaghetti.'

'That's good,' Enzio paused, and his face became serious, 'I am most troubled by the reports I have been getting. Most troubled indeed.'

Frank turned to stare out of the window. 'Everything's under control,' he said, his voice uptight.

'I wonder if Tomassio Vitorelli would agree with you,' Enzio replied mildly, then more harshly, 'we're not going to fuck about on this, Frank, I'm not here to get my rocks off.' He waved his arms about. 'We'll discuss it tonight after dinner, when Nick is here.'

'Sure,' Frank summoned a smile, 'sure, poppa, everything's going to be fine.'

Chapter 18

Dukey K. Williams was pleased. The hit on the *Magic Lantern* restaurant had been a big success. It had got rid of Tomassio Vitorelli, a big man in the Bassalino organisation, and it had put the fear of God into other restaurants and clubs who did not want the same treatment. Let the Bassalinos start to sweat. Let them begin to wonder. It was a good start.

Leroy Jesus Bauls was also pleased. It had been his idea.

Dukey K. Williams had come to him.

Dukey K. Williams was prepared to let Leroy do it his way.

Dukey K. Williams was going to lay a lot of bread on him, a lot of bread.

Sweet, everything was sweet for a guy who had started life with everything against him.

His Swedish mother was a hooker, and his

black father a pimp, and as soon as he was able he had left home. They were dead as far as he was concerned, and it wouldn't bother him one bit if they actually were.

Good-looking at an early age, Leroy never had any trouble finding a bed to sleep in, and if he wanted to follow his father's profession, there were plenty of offers. But Leroy had no desire to be beholden to any woman.

He joined a street gang, and cruised with them for a while. Small stuff, rolling drunks and old ladies, knocking off neighbourhood stores. By the time the profits were split up they were practically non-existent. Leroy knew he had to move on to better things.

He decided that narcotics was the business for him. He had smoked pot, tried acid twice. It did nothing for him. That was good. The thing to be in the narcotics business was cool, and definitely a non-participant. He had seen what drugs did to people, the way it affected their looks. He wanted none of that. But pushing was another bag of bones, pushing could lead to a lot of bread.

He knew people. He was young, good-looking, a convincing talker. He picked out the area he wanted to operate, and with a small stake from a friend he went into business.

He soon found he was stepping on toes. The area he had picked was already fully covered. They warned him off. He bought a gun with his first week's profits. They thought he was some punk kid, easy to handle.

There were three sets of toes he was stepping on. Within a month all three of them were dead, shot. Leroy's gun was wrapped in polythene, weighted with rocks, and safely laid to rest at the bottom of the river.

With his fifth week's profits he bought himself another one. He was sixteen years old.

For a year he concentrated solely on dealing. He worked on his own, with good sources of supply. He stashed his money away, and kept his gun handly. Nobody bothered him. He had a reputation. He kept to his own area, didn't get in anyone's way.

He lived alone in a rooming house. He never went out except on business. He rarely spent any money.

At the end of a year he had saved a substantial amount. Enough to buy a car, a whole new wardrobe of clothes, and rent a decent apartment.

He bought a black Mercedes, several black suits were specially made for him. He furnished his apartment with black leather.

He looked older than seventeen.

Leroy found with his new life style that he needed more money. So he employed two friends of his to work his area, and he moved on to new territory.

Within days he received word that Bosco Sam wanted to see him. Bosco Sam's toes were too many to step on and Leroy knew it, so he went to see him.

They came to an arrangement. Leroy was to keep to the area he already had, and instead of horning in on Bosco Sam's action, Bosco Sam would throw a couple of things his way that would bring him a lot more money than hustling drugs.

Leroy liked the idea. A lot more bread for a lot less work, and he still kept a couple of guys working his area.

In the first year Bosco Sam threw three contracts his way. Three hits. Leroy executed them all without a hitch. Leroy was moving up. He was getting himself a reputation, and it was doing him nothing but good in the world he had chosen to work in.

Now, four years later, Leroy Jesus Bauls was top man in his profession. He had long ago moved out of the drug scene.

He had used his spare time to study explosives, electronics, computer bombs. There was nothing he didn't know how to do, from blowing up a plane, to planting a bomb in a bank that would blow up three weeks later. He was a freelance hit man. The best.

Only he had a reputation for taking risks.

Every risk he had ever taken had paid off, and Leroy was riding high. Now he waited.

Dukey K. Williams would let him know when to move again and Leroy was ready.

Chapter 19

Angelo's apartment in Mayfair was small. A living-room, kitchen, bathroom. It was on the bedroom that he had splashed out. The walls were black and hung with leopard and tiger skins, the floor was carpeted in three-inch-thick fur, the ceiling was a kaleidoscope of different coloured mirrors. The bed dominated. It did everything electrically, from turning around in a slow circle, to producing television, stereo, or coffee at the touch of a button.

Angelo said proudly, 'You like the pad?'

Rio dismissed it with a glance. 'Get yourself a water bed, baby,' was her only comment.

They were both stoned. After Rio's initial introductory remark to Angelo, he had lost no time in getting rid of his little blonde companion and joining up with Rio's group. She was immediately cool, palming him off on Peaches, and making loud comments about Italian studs.

She was the centre of attention, outrageous in honky six-inch heel whore's shoes which raised her six-foot-height to ridiculous proportions. She towered over everbody. The thin, sinewy body undulating on the tiny packed dance floor in see-through cheesecloth—the sort of dress that gaped in places and was tied and swathed around her body. Silver bangles jangled halfway up both arms, and fertility symbols jostled and moved around her neck. Her make-up was extreme, and her long black Indian hair was coiled up and hidden under a purple Afro wig.

She danced with everyone, generating sexuality and excitement at high-level voltage. Angelo was content to hang around and watch, he knew that later she would go home with him. Her opening remark was the giveaway.

He sat back and enjoyed the show. He remembered a few years before. New York. He had been working for brother Frank, and one day he had been sent over to Billy Express's house to deliver a package. 'Personally,' Frank had said, 'only to him *personally.*'

Billy Express was not home, and Angelo had been told to wait. He was choked about it, he didn't like being a messenger boy. But then he heard the noises, unmistakable noises, and he went to investigate, soft-toed in the white sneakers he always chose to wear.

The noises were from the room next to the study where he had been told to wait. He opened the door a crack and peered in.

Rio and a Chinese man were on the floor. She was naked, spread-eagled, and above her the Chinese posed very still while she groaned loudly. Occasionally the Chinese moved, grinding himself deeply into her, withdrawing and then remaining motionless until the next short stab. It was driving Rio mad, and then suddenly she clutched at him, locking her long white legs round his neck and screaming with complete abandon.

Angelo closed the door quickly. He felt horny as hell, and as soon as he dropped the package to Billy Express he went over to Carita's house and dropped another load.

'That's four times this week,' Carita had complained, 'I told Frank you could have two freebee's a week, whadda ya think I am for chrissake? I'm running a business, not a frigging charity!'

The memory had always remained with Angelo. And now Rio Java was in London, in his apartment, and he was just as horny as the day he had delivered the package to Billy Express. Rio stretched, and with a couple of deft moves the dress fell off her. She wore nothing underneath, just the honky shoes and the wig. She was very thin, almost bony, almost flat-chested, with incredible black, hard nipples that extended right out. In the underground movie circles her nipples were quite famous, having been photographed by Billy Express from every angle. Her nipples were almost as famous as Andy Warhol's tin of Campbell's soup.

Angelo stripped off his clothes, anxious to keep up. He lowered the lights to a red glow, flicked on a James Brown tape.

Rio's eyes swept over him. 'Is that it?' she questioned, and then started to laugh.

Angelo smiled, not quite sure what she meant. He had a good hard-on, she couldn't mean him—he always received 'Oohs and aahs', not short, derisive laughs.

'Well now, little boy,' Rio said, 'where shall we begin?'

Angelo approached her. He wished that she would take the shoes off, without shoes they would be more or less the same height. The shoes gave her an advantage he didn't like. They made him feel small.

She was moving her body in time to the music, parting her legs, swaying back and forth to the funky sounds of 'Sex Machine'.

'Hey,' he said, 'take your shoes off.'

'But, honey, I like my shoes,' Rio drawled in an exaggerated Southern accent, 'they make me feel big and mean. All the better to gobble up naughty little boys like Angelo Bassalino.'

He gripped her by the waist.

'Show me your stuff super-stud,' she drawled.

They moved together.

'Get up—get on up—get up —get on up—get up—get on up—stay on the scene—get on up—like a sex machine.' Rio sang along with James Brown while Angelo's grip tightened and he moved her over to the bed. She was still singing as he pushed her back—'Get on up,' she chanted, 'get up—get it together—right on, baby.'

He mounted her, and before he knew what was happening she twisted her long legs straight out, trapping him inside her, and with one movement she strained her pelvis up and the pressure was so great, so incredibly tight, that he came at once.

She started to laugh, loud mocking laughter. The whole thing had taken a few seconds.

'Hey, baby,' she said, 'what are you—a rabbit?' She dissolved in more laughter while Angelo withdrew and tried to puzzle out what had happened. He had just moved inside her and that was it, a vice-like grip on his manhood that had pumped it all out of him in one fell swoop.

Rio was rolling about on the bed. 'How long's the intermission?' she complained, and with one hand she threw off the purple wig and shook the long, shiny black hair free.

To his credit Angelo was hard again. He prided himself on his control. He could go for hours if it was required. Mind over matter, that was the secret. And his mind had probably been dwelling on the first time he had seen her.

He moved over her breasts with his tongue. 'Let's fuck, baby,' she said briskly, 'that's what I'm here for. We can worry about the tongue jobs later.' She rolled on her stomach and he entered her from behind. When he was good and in she drew her legs together and raised herself a few inches. And again that incredible sensation, a tightness so relentless that he couldn't stop himself from coming, and it was a great come, a beautiful happening that no amount of mind over matter could stop.

'Jesus!' Rio exclaimed angrily, 'how long is it since you've been laid?'

Angelo was flaked out, he lay on the bed in a daze. He closed his eyes, five minutes of sleep and he'd feel strong again. James Brown sang 'It's A Man's Man's Man's World'. Angelo slept.

Smiling, Rio got up and dressed. It was a good start. She jammed on her wig, and danced around the room in her honky shoes humming softly to herself. Then in brown lipstick she wrote on the bathroom mirror YOU'VE GOT TO BE KIDDING!!

Then she left.

Chapter 20

Mary Ann August was delighted that Enzio had decided to bring her to New York with him. She would never admit it—well only to herself—but she found Miami tediously boring. It wasn't so much Miami, but the fact that she wasn't allowed out on her own, and the people who came to the house were all old. And then of course there was the woman peering out of the window all the time. It was very unnerving to have a pair of mad black eyes following you everywhere.

'Who is it?' Mary Ann had asked in alarm when she had first arrived.

'Forget it,' Enzio said briefly, 'just ignore her, and *never* let me catch your ass near that room.'

Mary Ann knew enough not to question him any further, but that didn't stop her talking to the maid who took meals into the room twice a day.

The girl was Italian and frightened to talk, but gradually Mary Ann pieced together the fact that it was Enzio's wife, and that she was mental and never left the room.

Mary Ann was scared, but as the weeks drifted into months, she forgot about the mad eyes and pretended that they weren't there. It was kind, she reflected, that Enzio had let the old bag stay and not shoved her into an institution.

Mary Ann wanted to do lots of things in New York. She wanted to buy some clothes, and go to some shows, and visit all the best restaurants.

Upon their arrival Enzio shut her in the hotel bedroom and told her to stay there until he said otherwise.

They had arrived in the morning, it was now seven in the evening and Mary Ann was bored, hungry and fed up.

She sat pouting on the bed, legs crossed, china-blue eyes glued to a quiz game on the television.

At first she didn't hear the knock on the door, and then Alio Marcusi came walking in.

'Oh, it's you,' she said, her voice sulky. 'Where's Enzio?'

Alio smiled. He had bathed and put on his

new blue suit. His few remaining hairs were plastered down with brilliantine. Enzio had given him the word. Mary Ann was out. There was a position for her in Los Angeles. Enzio always allowed Alio a turn when he was finished with a girl. It had always been that way, for thirty years it had been that way. Sometimes they objected, those were the ones that Alio liked best. At his age it was difficult to get it up in normal circumstances.

'He won't be coming,' Alio said mildly, 'I have a message for you . . .'

Chapter 21

There were candles on the table at Frank Bassalino's house, and the children washed, scrubbed, and in their best clothes, sat straight-backed at the table. Frank had given up his place at the head to his father, and he sat on his right. Anna Maria sat nervously opposite him.

Nick was there laughing and joking with the two younger children. He had not wanted to come, he had wanted to spend the whole evening with Lara. But Enzio had insisted, and Enzio was not a man you argued with.

Nick had arranged to meet Lara later, she hadn't minded, she had smiled and said, 'Of *course* I understand, family is family.' April would have ranted and raved for a week.

'Hey,' Enzio roared, 'Anna Maria makes the best spaghetti in town. You're a lucky man, Frank, a lucky man.' Enzio paused to belch loudly. 'Now I could give her a few little hints about the sauce—a touch more herbs—stronger wine . . .'

Anna Maria giggled nervously. Frank glanced up at Beth, she had come in the room to help the youngest child with his food. Her long hair was tied off her face, and she looked pale. He wondered how quickly Anna Maria would fall asleep, and how soon he could be with Beth. A nerve throbbed silently in his cheek. There would be business to discuss after dinner, it could turn out to be a long evening.

Later Enzio sent Anna Maria and the children from the room.

He sipped a small glass of Sambuca, and his eyes were fixed mostly on Frank as he spoke.

'It doesn't take long,' he said sourly, 'for the word to spread when you got no balls.'

'What?' said Frank, feeling the anger and frustration flood through his body.

'In our business, somebody throws a hit on you, you give it to them right back. You don't fuck around or hang about.'

'I've been trying to find out who's responsible.'

'Fuck that!' Suddenly Enzio was screaming, 'who cares who's responsible. Pile some action on *all* of them—with one of them you'll hit the dirt. Don't let no one shit on you Frankie

134

boy—you do and we'll all end up under the pile.'

Lara prowled around her apartment like a stranger. She hated the draped paisley fabric ceiling, the matching walls, the small round table with a collection of interesting miniature boxes.

She loathed the exotic plants climbing up the antique-mirrored hall. She couldn't stand the zebra throw rugs, the brown leather chairs.

The apartment had been done by a decorator, and the only place Lara felt at home was in the bathroom. Here, amongst the rows of make-up, mirrors, sprays, and brushes, she could relax.

The apartment had been decorated with a view to looking fabulous in the fashion magazines. And indeed it did. Lara had spent more time being photographed in it than in living there.

She decided that when the whole business with Nick was over she would sell it. It was pointless to surround yourself with somebody else's idea of good taste.

But when would the whole business with Nick be over? Wasn't it just beginning?

Sometimes Lara felt so confused. Was it going to work? Was the fact that April Crawford might blow Nick out going to affect him *that* much. And then after she had consoled him for a few weeks, when she dumped him, what then? Even if he was in a state, how was that really going to affect Enzio Bassalino?

Lara sighed. She wanted to help, and at the time Rio's idea of revenge had sounded perfect, but now . . . well Lara wasn't too sure any more. Maybe Dukey was right.

Lara dressed to meet Nick at *Le Club*. A black jersey snake of a dress with no back. A jewelled choker from Afghanistan, bracelets of thin beaten silver halfway up her arm.

Tonight was the night. Take him home to bed and keep him there until he read the morning gossip columns. The longer it took for him to call April the better.

Lara gave a short laugh. Margaret wouldn't have approved of what they were trying to do. Margaret would have been ashamed of them resorting to sex to get what they wanted.

The phone rang.

'Lara? Lara, is that you?'

'Oh, Alfa. How did you know I was here?'

'I call you every day,' Prince Alfa said indignantly, 'every day I try, every day no answer. How you think I feel?'

'I'm sorry. I had to go to the Coast.'

'But Lara, Lara,' he sighed, 'you could have phoned me.'

'I said I'm sorry,' Lara snapped.

'Well I have you now, so we forget it,' Prince Alfa decided arguing was not going to get him anywhere. 'You want I come there?'

'No.'

'Well then, you fly to me. Tomorrow. I meet you at Rome airport, then together we go to Gstaad for the backgammon.'

'No.'

'Lara, my beautiful. You make me very wild.'

'Give me a few more days. I'll join you in Gstaad then.'

'How many days?'

'Don't pin me down. Look, why don't you phone me tomorrow.' She hung up quickly and ignored the phone when it started to ring again.

Prince Alfa had been a spoilt bastard all his life, it would do him good to get a taste of his own medicine. Besides, she didn't want to be late for Nick.

Chapter 22

Angelo called Rio ten times before he finally got her.

'Hey,' he said, 'about the other night.'

'No apologies,' Rio said with a deep, throaty laugh, 'I understand, I'm a *very* understanding lady.'

'Can I see you tonight?'

'Listen, understanding I may be, but you and I just don't swing at the same pace.'

'The other night was a mistake,' Angelo said quickly. 'Look, I don't want to boast but...'

Rio cut him short. 'You're a sweet little horny guy, and great for teeny boppers and cute little ding-a-lings who want a fast ball— but sweetheart, you and I are in a different league.'

Angelo felt his whole reputation was at risk.
'Hey, I can explain the other night, it was . . .'

'Yeah, it was.' She hung up.

Angelo threw the phone down in anger. How
dare that great big freak put him down like
this. He wanted to see her, to show her. It was
a slight to have her think of him as a sexual
failure. He was a great ball. Countless women
had told him that. He could go for hours, he
had incredible control.

He picked up the phone and dialled his married lady friend. 'Come over right now,' he
snapped.

'I can't, one of the children is sick.'

He hung up, disgusted. Was he losing his
touch?

He dialled his female croupier friend. She
arrived within the hour and he rushed her into
bed. He gave her controlled action and countless orgasms for two hours. She screamed and
moaned her appreciation. He found he couldn't
come himself, and he was still hard when he
threw her out.

He phoned Rio again.

'You're very anxious,' she said, 'I don't like
anxious guys, it turns me off.'

'Can I come over?' he asked.

She consulted her watch, it was six o'clock.
'OK, be here in a minute.' She put the phone
down and went out.

Angelo waited outside her rented apartment
for an hour and there was no reply to his

constant ringing. He was pissed off. Who did she think she was?

He finally went to a nearby bar and had a few drinks. Then he phoned her and there was no reply.

He had another couple of Scotches. He didn't like drinking. Pot was his scene. By the time he got to the casino he was unsteady and belligerent, and Eddie Ferrantino sent him home.

He called up a girlfriend and took her to *Tramp*. Rio was there, surrounded by her so-called friends.

'You're a bitch,' he hissed at her.

'And you're a lousy lay,' she hissed back.

'Come home with me now and you'll eat your words,' he insisted.

'It's not words I'm interested in eating,' she said with a mocking stare.

'It's not words you'll get,' he mumbled.

He was obviously drunk. 'Let's go,' Rio said.

They took a taxi. Rio flung off her clothes as soon as they were into his apartment.

Angelo realised he had made a mistake. The booze had made him limp and groggy.

'Well?' Rio faced him, hand on her hips, legs apart. 'Get your clothes off, lover.'

She stripped him herself, and he couldn't even will himself into a hard-on. He was ashamed and sick.

She laughed at him. 'Call Momma when you grow up to be a big boy,' she jeered.

She dressed and left.

Chapter 23

It was late by the time Nick was through at his brother Frank's house. There had been much to discuss, so many problems. Nick didn't feel he was that much involved, things were running smoothly for him in California, the inside killings and takeovers in New York didn't really concern him.

'Putan!' Enzio spat at him when he said as much. 'What happens here today happens there tomorrow. You think you're protected by some guardian angel? Balls!'

Both Enzio and Frank were mad at him because he had flown in with no bodyguard.

'You don't *move* in New York unless you're covered,' Enzio had bellowed and Frank had immediately agreed. They dismissed the car and chauffeur Nick had engaged at the airport and replaced it with two of Frank's men. Nick wondered how Lara was going to feel about two heavies stationed outside her front door when they were together.

He was late arriving at *Le Club*. Lara was with a group of people who fortunately Nick did not know. She introduced him and he wished she hadn't. The fewer who knew who he was the better.

He looked around the club and didn't see any familiar faces. That was OK. Anyway he wasn't *alone* with Lara, it would be difficult to guess they were together. He had even arrived after her.

Nick relaxed a little. Lara looked beautiful as usual. He wanted to touch her, hold her. He was sick of only being with her at discothèques and parties.

'Let's go,' he whispered, fingering her leg under the table.

'You just got here,' Lara chided gently, 'it would be rude.'

'Listen,' his grip tightened on her leg, 'I don't give a fuck.'

'Don't you?' her voice was amused. 'My, how the climate changes your attitude. Let's dance.'

He didn't want to dance. He just wanted to get out of there.

Lara pulled him on the dance floor and pressed against him. He felt the excitement, the promise of what was to come. The hell with April, he was free, he wasn't married yet.

There was an Italian restaurant called *Pinocchios* in New York that reserved a king's welcome for Enzio Bassalino whenever he was in town. It was a family concern. Mother, father, two daughters and a son. They anticipated Enzio's needs and on any evening he was visiting, tables were given only to people he personally agreed to.

At one such table sat Kosta Gennas. A small, sweating man, with blackened teeth and gnarled-looking skin. It seemed incongruous that he should be sitting with the three most beautiful girls in the room.

He chewed on the end of a stubby cigar and sucked at his Scotch through a special silver straw.

No one at the table spoke. The girls, three different kinds of beauties, stared vacantly ahead. They all had old-fashioned, back-combed hairstyles, though each one had hair of a different shade. They were all large of bosom, long of leg.

Kosta Gennas jumped up abruptly when Enzio Bassalino entered. Enzio nodded briefly to him upon passing and it was not until an hour later that he summoned Kosta to join him at his table. 'I like the look of the blonde,' Enzio said, 'what's her story?'

'Nineteen years old,' Kosta replied quickly.

'Lovely girl, hard worker, only been with us two months. Married some bum, and when he left her decided there were better ways to make a living. We were saving her to send to Brazil, she'd be a sensation there. Of course when I heard you were looking we hung onto her...'

'Is she clean?' Enzio asked.

'Is she clean?' Kosta echoed in amazement, looking around in surprise at Enzio's six or seven male companions, 'he asks me if she's clean. Would I ever...'

'Enough,' said Enzio sharply. He didn't like Kosta Gennas, he never had. But Kosta always had the best girls, and he always knew exactly what would please Enzio. 'Send her over,' Enzio growled.

The girl came wobbling over on ridiculous high heels. She smiled nervously and Enzio indicated she should sit beside him. He looked her over closely. A pointed, pretty face, dominated by jammy, wide red lips. Green eye-shadowed grey eyes, a smattering of freckles that she had endeavoured to conceal. The figure was perfect.

'What's your name, dear?' Enzio asked kindly.

'Miriam,' she whispered, in a Marilyn Monroe copy voice.

'Well, Miriam,' Enzio said, his eyes greedily devouring her ample cleavage, 'how would you feel about coming to live in my house in Miami?'

* * *

Anna Maria set her alarm clock for six a.m. every day. Then, heavy with child, she would stumble in the dark to the kitchen, where she liked to sit and drink warm, sweet tea, and watch the morning grow light. She had never trusted anyone else to make the children's breakfast. She liked to do it herself, mix the hot, lumpy porridge, heat the bread, set out the home-made plum jam. By seven, when they all appeared, Anna Maria always had everything ready.

She was a strong girl, but after four pregnancies her legs were feeling weak, her belly stretched almost beyond control. She was hoping the birth would be soon. Frank went off her when she was pregnant. He never touched her, he avoided looking at her. He never said anything, but she knew, and it saddened her. After all it was he who wanted many children.

Anna Maria struggled into her dressing-gown. She was exhausted, hopefully today would be the day. It had been hectic entertaining Enzio, there had been so much extra cooking to do, preparing all his favourite dishes. The children more excitable than usual, Frank, surly and nervous. It seemed almost as if she had just got into bed, and now it was another day.

She plodded wearily into the kitchen, switched the light on, and stared with a sense of unreality at her husband, Frank. He crouched over Beth who leaned back across the kitchen table. His face was creased, and his breath short. He still wore his clothes, but Beth was naked, a crumpled white nightgown by her feet.

Anna Maria's hand fled to the crucifix that she wore around her neck, and her eyes wide with hurt she started to mumble in Italian.

'Jesus Christ!' Frank bellowed. He was nearly at the moment of climax. Beth wriggled away from him too soon, and his milky white semen fell to the kitchen floor. The final insult. 'You bitch,' he screamed at Anna Maria, 'spying on me, you fucking little bitch!' His face was red with rage.

Anna Maria turned to run, but it was too late, Frank was after her, his arm raised, his anger uncontrollable. As he struck her she fell to the floor and he stood over her, his arm raised to give her more.

Beth could not believe what was happening. She hadn't meant it to be like this. When she had changed the time on Anna Maria's alarm clock she had intended that they be discovered, but she had not realised that Frank would turn into a screaming madman.

For a moment she was paralysed. And then the full realisation of what he was doing to his wife hit her, and she threw herself at him, trying to hold his angry, flailing arms back, begging him to stop.

It seemed to come to him suddenly what he was doing, and he stopped.

'Oh, my God,' he groaned, 'oh, my God!'

Anna Maria was still, and for a moment Beth feared she might be dead. But she listened and heard faint breathing, and without a word to Frank she phoned for an ambulance.

Frank was crying, and trying to cradle Anna Maria in his arms when the ambulance arrived.

'She fell down the stairs,' he told the ambulance men.

They exchanged glances. They had heard that one before.

Then Anna Maria started to groan. Horrible loud animal groans.

'Get her to the hospital quick,' Beth said urgently, 'I think she's going to have the baby!'

Chapter 24

Leroy Jesus Bauls watched the ambulance pull
up at Frank Bassalino's house with hardly a
flicker of interest showing in his flat eyes. He
was chewing gum, slowly, methodically. Now
he took the gum from his mouth, squeezed it
into a tight, hard ball and rolled it between his
fingers.

How easy it would be to lay a hit on Frank
Bassalino. One carefully aimed shot between
the eyes, it would be a cinch. By the time the
two goons who were apparently his protection
reacted, Leroy Bauls would be long gone.

He was an easier hit than the old man. Enzio
Bassalino knew what protection was all about,
and where he moved he was always surrounded
and shielded. Of course he protected himself in

an old-fashioned way, there were so many other methods to catch him by.

Leroy yawned. It was a shame there was nothing to be done. But he knew his home-work, and if the occasion should arise. If Dukey K. Williams should give the word for the final hit...

He dropped the chewing gum to the ground. He had work to do. The Bassalinos were prov-ing to be a stubborn family, but they would learn...

Leroy walked slowly back to the van he had rented. He wore cheap clothes with 'Samons Linens' written across the T-shirt he had on. Once in the van he jammed on a black leather cap, and yellow-tinted shades.

He smiled tightly. He could hear the wit-nesses now. 'Yeah—a black boy—about twenty something—tall—skinny—how the hell do I know what he looked like—he was *black*.'

'We all look alike baby,' Leroy muttered, 'beautiful!'

He drove the van carefully. It wouldn't do to have a little smash up, it wouldn't do at all.

Barberellis was a large Italian restaurant and bar situated on a main street. Leroy pulled the van up directly outside and got out. He took a large laundry basket from the back of the van and carried it with difficulty inside.

A girl was sitting behind a cash register doing sums, and a wizened old man beat at the floor listlessly with a broom.

'Morning,' Leroy sang out, 'Samons Linens, fresh delivery. Anything to go?'

The girl looked up vaguely. She had only worked there a week. 'I don't know,' she said, 'nobody's in yet. You'd better leave it on a table.'

'Sure.' Whistling, Leroy chose a table by the window. The old man didn't look up. 'I'll drop by tomorrow,' Leroy said.

'OK,' the girl replied, uninterested. Still whistling, Leroy departed.

He was three blocks away when he heard the explosion.

It gave him a strange, almost sensual jolt of pleasure. Carefully he extracted a new piece of gum from the pack, and even more carefully he drove the van to his next stop.

Manny's was a nightclub, and the front was all closed up. Leroy took the laundry basket from the car and made his way round the back. It was open, there seemed to be no one around. He carried the basket past several dirty-looking dressing-rooms, through the dance floor, and placed it on a table.

He was starting to perspire slightly, the basket was heavy, and there wasn't that much time. As he turned to leave, a door from the Ladies' Room swung open, and a voice said, 'Hey, boy, what you think you doin' here?'

Leroy smiled. 'Samons Linens,' he said.

The woman waddled forward. She was fat and elderly, obviously the cleaning lady, and with her she had a small, bright-eyed child. The thing that bothered Leroy was the fact they they were both black.

'We don't deal with no Samons Linens,' the old woman said, 'so's you all can get that basket outta here fast as you all got it in—boy.'

Leroy glanced at his watch. Time was running short.

Shit! A voice screamed in his head. Shit! Shit! Shit! Be smart and get your ass *out*, the voice told him. But he couldn't leave them. They were his people. Black didn't kill black.

'Well, M'am,' Leroy said calmly, 'if you will be good enough to step outside with me, maybe you can tell that to the driver.'

The woman viewed him suspiciously, then she said to the child, 'You stay here, Vera May. Don't you touch nothin', you hear?'

Leroy thought quickly. Tell them the truth? No, the old woman wouldn't believe him. Anyway there wasn't time. On impulse he scooped the child up and started to run back the way he had come in. The child began to scream. Leroy glanced back. Waving her arms in a panic the old woman was following them.

In his head he began the countdown—sixty, fifty-nine, fifty-eight. There would be no time to take the van now. The van would go up with the rest of the building. Forty-five, forty-four, forty-three. Outside at last.

'Shut up,' he muttered to the kid. The old

woman would be out soon. Get at least a block away.

He ran down the street clutching the child, and behind him he heard the screams of the old woman. 'Stop that man, stop him—he's got my Vera May, my baby!'

Passers-by stared at him, but nobody tried to stop him. This was New York, people were not fools.

At the corner he paused, any second now. He placed the child on the pavement. 'You stay right there,' he said and in the distance he saw the woman getting closer.

He sprinted off in the direction of the underground, annoyed at his own foolishness.

Then loud and clear came the rumblings of the explosion. He glanced back. The woman and child were together, frozen, while people around them ran back towards the noise.

Leroy ducked down the stairs to the subway. In the Men's Room he got rid of the Samons Linens T-shirt, the hat and shades.

It had been a good morning's work. It would certainly show the Bassalino family a thing or two. And Dukey K. Williams would be more than pleased.

Chapter 25

Angelo didn't know what it was. It was a feeling that twisted his gut and stayed in his head. Rio Java. Rio Java. All he could think about was Rio Java.

Was this love? he thought to himself bitterly. This couldn't be love, this nagging, persistent obsession. She wasn't a beautiful woman, she wasn't even a particularly young woman. She was just a freak. A six-foot-two, randy, Red Indian freak.

He made up his mind to forget her.

His father phoned from New York. There was trouble all over, there had been certain threats. It was best that Angelo didn't go around unprotected.

'Ah, come on,' Angelo argued. His father talked like an old gangster movie.

'Read the papers, you stupid little bastard, there's hits happening everywhere. You're my son, that makes you an important bit of bargaining property. I'm having the Stevestos assign a man to you.'

Angelo groaned, 'Listen . . .'

'No, you listen. I hear reports of you being drunk, bumming around. Straighten your ass or I'll haul you back here. You want that?'

Angelo swallowed an angry reply. He liked it in London. The more distance between himself and his family the better as far as he was concerned.

A man called Shifty Fly was commissioned to protect him. It annoyed Angelo that he had to be followed and accompanied everywhere.

Shifty Fly looked like his name. Thin, watery, darting eyes, a sweating shoulder holster concealing a gun beneath the crabby grey suit he always wore.

'This is a joke,' Angelo complained to Eddie Ferrantino.

Eddie flicked cold eyes over him and marvelled yet again that this bearded little jerk could possibly be Enzio Bassalino's son. 'Just do as your father says, be a good little boy.'

Bullshit on the 'little boy' jazz. Angelo was sick and tired of it. First Rio and now Eddie. Who the hell did they think they were?

He took out his various girlfriends and gave

it to them regularly. There were no complaints.
He forced himself not to contact Rio. She was a
bad scene, and even he knew enough not to ask
for more.

He lasted a week, and then he called her.

'Hey, Rio, this is Angelo.'

'Angelo who?'

Bitch! 'Angelo Bassalino.'

'Let me see now, I don't think I remember an
Angelo Bassalino . . .'

He laughed nervously, 'Stop kidding around.
I thought you might like dinner.'

'I always like dinner. In fact I have it every
night. Do you have it every night?'

'Yes.'

'Then why don't you run off and have it
now.' And she hung up.

He sent her flowers, something he had *never*
done. She sent them back when they were dead
with a note, 'Hey—isn't it funny—does everything you handle go limp?'

He found that although he was quite able to
service all his girlfriends it was virtually impossible for him to reach a climax. Always he
remained hard as a rock, ready to go for ever. It
was causing him great physical discomfort.
When the hard-on vanished he was left with a
pain in his gut that lasted all night.

Apart from the aggravation of that, there
was Shifty Fly always close at hand. Foul
mouthed and slimy he trailed Angelo everywhere.

* * *

Rio was pleased with the way things were going. She had always had the power of grabbing men by the balls sexually. Larry Bolding had been one of the few exceptions, and that was because he was shit scared of his wife, political career, and his spotless reputation.

Boy, could she blow the whistle on his spotless reputation. One of these days, baby, one of these days . . .

It had been a week since she had sent the flowers back to Angelo. The time was ripe. She picked up the phone and called him. He was asleep.

'Yeah?' said a muffled voice.

'Listen you,' said Rio, 'don't you think it's about time I taught you how to ball?' There was silence from him. Rio continued, 'Last chance, sweetheart. Bag your ass over here quick and I'll show you some tricks you ain't never gonna forget!' She hung up.

Angelo struggled awake. It was past midnight. He threw on some clothes and left by the back entrance. This was one scene Shifty Fly wasn't going to be following him to.

Chapter 26

Lara paced her living-room smoking nervously. It was early with the light just seeping through the darkness, New York taking shape outside.

Why had she ever become involved in this?

Nick was asleep in the bedroom. Why did it have to be Nick?

Her hand was shaking slightly, her cheeks were flushed, her hair tangled. She didn't want to take it any further. Nick was not responsible for things his father did. Dukey K. Williams had been right, and Rio with her far-out plans all wrong. Much as she had loved Margaret, she was dead, and there was no method or plan or revenge that could bring her back. If Enzio Bassalino was the man to blame, then let Dukey deal with him in the way he wanted to.

They had left *Le Club* at three that morning. 'Your place or my hotel?' Nick had questioned.

She had felt light-headed. 'My place.'

They had started to kiss in the car, necking like a couple of high-school kids.

'I am hot for you, sugar,' and he had guided her hand down to the bulge in his trousers that lent truth to his statement.

She started to feel guilty that she was actually enjoying the whole scene. But her guilt was swept away in his arms, as he ripped the six-hundred-dollar black dress off her, and made love to her on the floor of her apartment.

Later they went in the bedroom, and it had happened two more times before she fell asleep.

How was it possible to fall in love with someone you were supposed to hate?

'How about some coffee, princess?' Nick came walking in. He was naked. His body lean and hard and tanned. He put his arms around her and hugged her close, and slowly he undid the buttons of her housecoat, pushing it off her shoulders, sliding it down her body.

She sighed, leaning her head back to catch his kisses. It had never been this way with anyone before, this pure physical pull. There had always been reasons why she had gone to bed with people, hard-hitting, down-to-earth reasons. With Nick it wasn't like that. Oh, there was the reason all right, but it didn't matter, it wasn't important.

Nick was carrying her back to the bedroom. 'You are beautiful,' he was saying, 'beautiful! Beautiful! Beautiful!'

She held on to him tightly. Soon the morning papers would be arriving. She wondered how he would feel then.

Beth stayed with the Bassalino children. She felt sick at what she had done. If anything happened to Anna Maria's baby . . .

Frank phoned in the morning. His voice sounded funny. 'Pack up and get out of there,' he told Beth, 'do it *now*. I don't want to find you there when I get back.'

'Is everything all right?' Beth asked, 'the baby?'

There was silence for a minute, and then Frank's voice harsh and loud. 'Get out of my house, and don't leave no forwarding address 'cos if I ever set eyes on you again I'll kill you.' He slammed the phone down and Beth started to shake.

It was over. Whatever it was it was over. She was free. She could go.

She picked up the phone and dialled enquiries. They gave her the number of the hospital. She knew what they would tell her, but she had to be sure.

'Mrs Frank Bassalino, admitted early this morning. I'm a relative. Is she doing well?'

The operator's voice was apologetic. 'I'm

sorry, we cannot give information over the phone.'

Beth ran to her room and packed her few things. She left the children with the maid. She stepped outside the house and felt relief at leaving sweep over her like a cool breeze.

She took a bus to the hospital. She was frightened of bumping into Frank, but the fear was overcome by a need to know what had happened.

'Mrs Bassalino died at eight a.m.,' a nurse told her, 'complications with the position of the baby, and other things . . .' the nurse trailed off. 'Are you a close friend? I think Doctor Rogers might care to speak to you.'

'And the baby?'

'Everything possible was done, but I'm afraid . . .'

Beth turned and ran.

The nurse started after her. 'Please wait, if you can help us at all . . .'

Beth kept running. She didn't stop running until she reached Grand Central station. She bought herself a ticket home. Before boarding the train she phoned Cass. 'I guess it's what you all wanted,' she said bitterly, 'but how does it help Margaret? It certainly doesn't bring her back.'

Chapter 27

They were balling.

'You're getting better all the time,' Rio laughed, 'maybe I was wrong about you.'

Angelo felt very relaxed. He was in control. Like a car that has been perfectly tuned he rode the crest of each bump and hill and didn't falter.

The Stones mumbled hornily on background stereo. It was early evening and things had been going successfully all afternoon.

'I think we'll take a break for food,' Rio announced, 'got a friend who'll bring over marvellous goodies.'

She rolled away from him and lifted the phone. Angelo lay back. He felt so good, he was still hard after hours of activity.

'See you soon,' Rio was purring into the phone. 'Sure, bring Peaches, I'm certain there's plenty to go around.' Rio flopped back on the bed, 'Food will be here soon, meanwhile how about an appetiser?'

Angelo thought about phoning the casino to let them know he wouldn't be in tonight, but what the hell, it would only bring Shifty Fly running to station himself outside, and who needed that?

Rio liked popping ammis, and she was fixing another one and smothering it under his nose. He breathed deeply, deeply. 'You know you're not too bad,' Rio muttered, 'but Jesus Christ your beard is itchy.'

Enzio paced the private room at the hospital, his face was grim.

Frank sat in a chair, his head buried in his hands.

Enzio muttered in Italian, occasionally throwing words of disgust in his son's direction.

Dr Rogers came in, a weary, bespectacled young man, with receding hair and sinewy, nervous hands.

Enzio clapped him round the shoulders. 'Doctor, we know you did all you could, you mustn't blame yourself.'

Dr Rogers shook himself away. 'I don't blame myself,' he said indignantly, 'I don't blame myself at all.' He turned to stare at

Frank, 'I'm afraid that poor girl was very badly beaten, the baby had no chance, it was . . .'

'She fell down the stairs,' Frank mumbled, 'I told you that before, she fell.'

'Mr Bassalino, your wife's internal injuries were not consistent with falling down some stairs. She was beaten and that's what will have to go on the death certificate,' he stared with contempt at Frank, 'I'm sure there will be an enquiry.'

Enzio approached the doctor. 'Are you a family man?' he enquired.

'Yes,' the doctor said shortly.

'Pretty wife? Nice kiddies?'

'I don't see what this has to do . . .'

'Plenty,' Enzio said. 'As a family man you can understand the occasional little tiff, lovers' quarrel. My boy is a man suffering, you want to make it worse for him?'

'Mr Bassalino, I have a duty to perform.'

'Of course, of course, and I'm not trying to stop you. I think you doctors do a wonderful job, and yet so underpaid, terrible, a crime. Hardly enough to keep your wife looking pretty,' Enzio paused, 'you know what I mean huh? I'm an old man, but I still appreciate a pretty face, it would be a shame if your wife lost hers.' Enzio fumbled in his pocket, producing a wad of bills carefully held together with an elastic band. 'Here's a thousand dollars, doctor, to help you out.'

Dr Rogers hesitated as Enzio thrust the money towards him.

'Take it,' Enzio said, his voice mild, 'keep your wife pretty.'

By the time the papers were delivered Nick had fallen back to sleep.

Lara scanned them quickly. In the gossip column of one was the item she had known would be there. The writer was a bitchy woman columnist and she had put it together as only a bitch could.

How does glamorous star of the forties, still frisky April Crawford do it? Married four times, those in the know say she is about to take El plungo five with handsome thirtyish Nick Bassalino, a Los Angeles businessman. However, someone should tell Nick, for when last seen he was boarding a plane for New York with gorgeous, beautiful Lara Crichton, a stunning jet setter of twenty-six. Last report had them dancing cheek to cheek amongst other things at New York's chic-est discothèque, *Le Club*.

There was a picture of Lara taken in Acapulco and used in *Vogue*. She looked incredible. And a picture of April leaving a film première looking tired.

Oh well, that was goodbye to April. She

would never stand for this. But where did it leave Lara?

It wasn't fair. She hadn't known it would be like it was. She hadn't reckoned on actually liking him. He was so very different from all the men she had ever known, so very masculine, and sexual. There was nothing phony about him. He was just as he was.

She took the paper in the bedroom and tossed it at him. 'I don't think you're going to like this,' she said flatly.

Rio had fixed fantastic drinks. Rum, brown sugar, eggs, cream, Benedictine, all mixed together in the blender. When the doorbell rang she told Angelo to stay in bed, she would get it. Naked except for the honky shoes she always liked to wear, she marched off.

What with the ammis and the sex and the couple of joints they had had, and the heavy drink, he felt pretty tired. Pleasantly so. Christ, she couldn't object to him falling asleep now. There could be no more name calling, he had proved himself at last.

He closed his eyes. He felt a bit strange, a bit suspended. More than being stoned, almost like his mind was leaving his body and drifting over to the corner to watch him. That was funny. That was really funny, and he started to laugh, but his laugh wasn't coming out of his mouth, it was coming out from all over, his nose, ears, even his ass. The thought only made him laugh more, and the more he laughed the more strange sensations became.

There seemed to be a lot of people coming into the room. Nice smiling faces who appreciated his laughter.

They were taking off their clothes and the clothes were floating around the room in slow motion, and he was too tired to get up from the bed, but he was enjoying himself. He was having such a *good* time.

'Hey, baby,' Rio's face focused very near to his, 'you remember Hernando and Peaches. They *both* want to meet you.'

Her voice saying 'meet you' echoed and echoed round the room until it became like an Indian *mantra*. He nodded his head and it seemed to leave the rest of his body and bob around the room.

Hernando was laying strong hands on him, caressing his sex, taking it in his mouth, and Angelo groaned with pleasure. His penis felt bigger than his body. His body was nothing.

Peaches was exquisite, a fine-boned Slavic face with thick blonde hair, pushing Hernando away and taking over.

Somewhere Rio's laughter hung heavy in the air.

They turned him over and Hernando mounted him and he knew it was a man forcing his way inside, but it didn't matter, it didn't matter at all. In fact, it was great, and Peaches was taking him in her mouth at the same time and he thought he was reaching a pinnacle of eternity, and the actual coming was an explosion that rivalled with the Atomic bomb. Pow!! Great mushroom clouds. And he drifted off into the sleep he had been waiting for.

Chapter 28

Nick argued impatiently with April Crawford's maid on Lara's bedroom telephone. 'Now come on, Hattie, I *know* she's there. Tell her again, I *have* to talk to her, it's *very* important.'

Hattie lowered her voice, 'Mr Bassalino, it's just no good. She has locked herself in her room and won't talk to anyone.'

'You're sure you told her it's me?'

'*Especially* you she won't talk to.'

'Oh shit, Hattie, you know what she's like. I'll try and get a plane back today. How many bottles has she got in there with her?'

'*Mr Bassalino!*' Hattie exclaimed in shocked tones. She had been with April nineteen years and still refused to admit to the fact that she drank.

'Keep an eye on her Hattie, talk to her, tell her not to believe everything she reads in the papers. I'll probably see you tonight.'

Lara, who had been hovering outside, came into the room brightly. 'Well,' she said, forcing a smile, 'that's it then, is it?'

'What?' Nick said shortly.

'Running back to momma's arms. Hope she'll forgive you for being bad.'

Nick shook his head sadly, 'Lara—Lara. I'm surprised at you.'

He's surprised *at me!* Lara thought angrily. Jesus, but she had been acting like a naïve idiot. Blinded by one night of good sex. She had honestly expected him to *want* to stay, but all he wanted to do was run back to April.

'When are you leaving?' she asked coldly.

'I don't know, I have to call my father.'

'Oh, I see. Can't go unless daddy says so. Well, if he says you have to stay over another night, shall we have a repeat performance? After all we're both here, it would be silly not to take advantage of that.'

'Listen,' Nick said, getting off the bed, still naked, 'don't talk like a cunt, it doesn't suit you. You knew what this was going to be. You knew about me and April. I *love* April Crawford, like I'm going to *marry* her.'

'Don't be insulting,' Lara was close to tears, 'just get dressed and go.'

Nick shrugged. 'If it means anything to you, last night was Wonderland.'

'It did mean something to me, it doesn't any more.'

He tried to take her in his arms but she shook free.

'Are you coming back to Los Angeles?' he asked.

'With you?' she said sarcastically.

'You know what I mean.'

'No, I'm not.'

'When will I see you again?'

Lara laughed. 'God, Nick, you're really too much. In one breath it's how you love April Crawford and you're going to marry her. And in the next it's when will you see me again. Well you won't not ever.'

He shook his head, 'Don't count on it.'

Golli and Segal arrived at the hospital and took Frank home. 'Don't leave him,' Enzio warned, 'stay with him all the time.'

Enzio had made all the arrangements for the funeral. He had spoken to Anna Maria's family still in Sicily. Her mother and sister would fly in for the funeral arranged for two days' time.

Enzio was sick to his stomach concerning Frank. To beat a pregnant woman . . . God knows it was a terrible thing to do. But thank God that it had happened while Enzio himself was in New York and able to deal with matters so that there was no disgrace brought upon the family. Still, Enzio had never expected anything like this from Frank, his eldest, and he had thought most dependable, boy.

He would be punished. God would punish him for such a sin. Enzio firmly believed in the power of the Almighty for certain things.

What a morning! News of the bombings at *Manny's* and *Barberelli's* had reached Enzio. It was those black bastards. They were responsible. A show of strength was needed, but Christ what strength could you show to a bunch of maniacs who walked around in broad daylight blowing up places? Enzio knew there had to be an answer. There had to be or the whole Bassalino organisation's reputation would be at risk. Who would pay protection for no protection?

He had been trying all morning to telephone Angelo in London. Where was the stupid boy? It was a worry—yet another worry Enzio did not need at his age. Angelo had not appeared at the casino and had managed to disappear without his bodyguard.

Enzio swore as yet again the overseas operator told him there was no reply at the number. He knew what he would do when he got him. He would bring him home for Anna Maria's funeral, and he would keep him home. No more screwing around in London. Maybe he would put him to work for Frank again, he should be close to the family where he could be watched.

Nick arrived at the hotel.

'What took you so long?' Enzio snapped. 'You should have come to the hospital.'

'I only just heard. What happened?'

Enzio shrugged sadly. 'An accident, she fell down the stairs.'

'Fell down the stairs? How? Where was Frank? Jesus, it just seems unbelievable.'

Enzio nodded. 'I know, I know. She was pregnant, clumsy on her feet. A terrible accident.'

'She was such a sweet kid...'

'And you?' Enzio suddenly bellowed, 'where the fuck were you all night? I need you, no one can find you.' Enzio shook his head, 'Don't you have no sense Nick? These are dangerous times.'

'I called the hotel soon as I got up,' Nick said defensively, 'then I broke my balls rushing over here.'

'You broke your balls last night,' Enzio commented dryly. 'At least it's good you can forget about the old piece you screw in Hollywood. No time for talk now, you go to your brother's house and stay with him.'

'I should be getting back to the Coast, without me things can start...'

'Enough!' Enzio shouted, 'I don't understand my children. Your brother loses his wife—*your* sister-in-law. There should be tears in your eyes, but no, he mumbles about getting back to the Coast. Ha! You go to Frank's house, you stay with him, you comfort him. You'll stay in New York until after the funeral.'

'When's that?'

'Don't question me!' Enzio screamed. 'Get out of here.' His heart was bouncing around, a sign of overexertion no doubt. God, what had he done to deserve three idiot sons?

Chapter 29

Dukey K. Williams accepted the news of the bombings with good humour. He congratulated Leroy.

Lately Dukey went over to see Cass. 'I want to leave the apartment,' he told her.

The apartment he had shared with Margaret had originally belonged to her, and when she was murdered Dukey had told Cass he wanted to stay there, so Cass had made suitable arrangements.

Now he wanted to forget the past.

When Margaret's death was avenged he wanted to be ready to move on.

Cass told him about Anna Maria Bassalino, and Beth's return to the commune.

He shrugged, 'I told you she should never have gotten involved.'

Cass agreed.

'Pull the other two out,' Dukey warned, 'I'm taking over now, I'm doing it my way, and I don't want them fuckin' around screwin' things up.'

Dukey then called his manager and said, 'Get the show on the road again, baby, I'm gonna be ready to work in a week.'

His manager was delighted.

Dukey then called Leroy. 'Let's cut the shitting around. Start with Frank at the funeral and then the house. I don't want to hang around any longer. Your plan. The bread will be waiting.'

Chapter 30

Angelo found it difficult forcing his eyes to open, but he managed it. He blinked several times, his eyes felt crusty, and bloodshot. He was alone on Rio's bed in Rio's apartment. The curtains were closed, so that he wasn't sure if it was night or day.

His body ached, and there was an uncomfortable, unfamiliar feeling about his backside.

'Jesus Christ!' he sat up slowly, gingerly. What the hell had happened to him?

He remembered clearly coming to the flat. He remembered Rio greeting him. He remembered the great scene they had had. He remembered the ammis, the pot, the drinks. Then it was a blank. One long—how long?—blank.

It must have been the drinks. The thick, creamy, fantastic drinks that Rio had dipped her fingers in and fed him with.

Where was Rio anyway?

He got up, aware of the difference in his body, beginning to be much more aware of how it must have happened.

He had to pee. He went to the bathroom. Taped on the mirror were six colour Polaroids. They left him in no doubt as to what had happened. In case he was not convinced Rio had lipsticked on the mirror—RIGHT ON BABY! I ALWAYS KNEW YOU WERE A FAG.

He stared at the pictures. They were of him and a plumpish, dark man, and a beautiful blonde girl, only she wasn't a girl, she couldn't be a girl, because in spite of the breasts she had a penis.

Angelo had always feared men getting close to him. He was revolted when touched by them, even a friendly back pat annoyed him. He had scrupulously avoided any homosexual experiences. Now this. And in the pictures he was smiling, laughing, actually *enjoying* it.

God Almighty, if anyone saw these pictures. If his *father* should see them.

Hurriedly, he ripped them off the mirror and tore them into small pieces. He flushed the bits down the toilet.

He took a deep breath. With the evidence gone he felt much better.

What was he worried about? He wasn't a fag,

half of the ladies in London could testify to that.

It was Rio's fault. Where the hell was she? He looked round the apartment. It was empty. She must have planned the whole scene.

Well, he wasn't going to let her get away with it, he would think of *some* form of retaliation that would blow her cool.

Nick had gone. Lara was keyed up and nervous. Things had gone the way she had planned, but then again they hadn't.

What if April did take him back? It wasn't a likely prospect, but what if she did? Then it would all have been useless.

But would it? Was it useless that she had finally met a man who could make her feel emotions other than how big his bank balance was, or what his title was?

Was it useless that she had enjoyed having sex for the first time in years?

Was it useless that she had fallen in love for the first time ever?

Anyway it didn't matter, Lara had made up her mind. Whatever happened she was through. She did not want to be involved any more. She never wanted to set eyes on Nick Bassalino again. She would call Cass and tell her so, and then she would call Prince Alfa in Rome or wherever he was, and tell him to come and fetch her.

* * *

Nick went to Frank's house. The children were whiny and noisy.

'Where's the nanny?' Nick enquired.

'Gone,' Frank mumbled. He was drinking neat whisky, hunched in a chair, his eyes bloodshot, his whole appearance unruly.

'Jesus, Frank, I'm sorry about everything . . .' Nick tailed off. He had never been very close to his brother. When they were kids Frank used to beat the shit out of him. Frank had always been the biggest and the strongest and the best in everything.

Nick wandered into the room where Golli and Segal were watching television. It was such a depressing house. Old and worn. It was a house that must have looked the same twenty, even thirty years previously. Nick thought with longing of his own place in Los Angeles. Big and spacious. White and modern. He thought of April's house, rambling and beautiful, with the lake in the garden, and the swimming pool in the living room. California was the only place for him, with the climate and the people. The relaxed way of living. You could stick New York. Dirty pavements and uptight people. Everyone white-faced and hustling.

He went upstairs and placed another call to April. It was the same story. He told Hattie he was delayed, and why. 'Be sure to tell her why,' he emphasised. Christ, April was liable to think he was hanging around to be with Lara.

Thinking of Lara, it had been nice, she was a very lovely lady. But beautiful girls were a plague in Los Angeles. You fell over them everywhere you went. April Crawford was an original. A true star. Nick was confident that she would forgive him. He would explain, nothing to it. Lara just happened to be on the same plane—coincidence—it could happen to anyone. And April better than anyone would understand about the gossip columns—pure hokum—who ever believed them?

Yes, Nick was sure everything would work fine.

He wondered what Lara was doing. He wondered if she would hang up if he called her.

Nope. Best to forget her.

He had wanted her. He had had her. End of story. Christ, it was going to be boring, hanging around the house with Frank.

'Hey, Segal,' Nick said, 'how about a game of gin? Any cards around this mausoleum?'

Chapter 31

Mary Ann August woke up in Los Angeles. She couldn't remember much about getting there, after Alio Marcusi had slobbered all over her, there had been another visitor, a woman called Claire.

Mary Ann could remember being frightened and telling Claire that when Enzio found out what had happened to her there would be plenty of trouble. Claire had laughed, and called her honey. 'Don't worry, honey, Enzio knows all about it, he wants you to come on a little journey with me.'

Then Claire had stuck a needle into her arm, making her groggy and docile, and she had dressed and left the hotel with Claire, and there had been a car journey, then an aeroplane, another car trip, and then a house, a room, sleep. Now she was awake.

She got up. She was in a bedroom, a plain room with olive green walls and shuttered windows. The shutters wouldn't open, nor would the door.

She peered at herself in a mirror. Her back-combed hair was sad and straggly, her make-up streaked and faded.

Nothing annoyed Mary Ann more than not looking well. She searched for her purse and found it on the floor, then painstakingly she applied fresh make-up and redid her hair. When the job was finished, she wondered where on earth she was, and what was happening.

During her six months with Enzio, Mary Ann had acquired quite a few possessions. Jewellery, clothes, a mink coat, and of course her latest acquisition—the full-length Chinchilla.

It was of these things she was thinking now. They were her protection when Enzio finally got tired of her. They would buy her a decent future so that she didn't have to go back to dancing around naked on a stage for a living.

The woman Claire came into the room. She was fortyish, and slim, a little bit masculine.

'I don't understand,' Mary Ann said, 'where's Enzio? Why does he want me here?'

Claire smiled. 'He thought you needed a change. He thought California might do you good. He knows I have a lot of nice friends here, and he thought it would do you good to meet some of them.'

'Well, why didn't he tell me?'

Claire put her arm across Mary Ann's shoulders. 'Enzio told me one of your best qualities was that you didn't ask a lot of questions. You're a very pretty girl, but that hair-style will have to go.'

'Enzio likes my hair this way.'

'Enzio won't be here for a while . . .'

'What about my things? My clothes and jewellery and my fur coats?'

'Don't worry about them. Enzio's having them sent. Be a good girl and co-operate with me and everything will be fine.'

Dumb as she was, Mary Ann was slowly beginning to realise that all was not well.

Chapter 32

Shifty Fly saw Angelo safely aboard the big jumbo jet bound for New York. 'Don't think it hasn't been fun,' he sneered.

'Listen, man,' Angelo said, 'don't get so uptight, you've got your job to do. It's just that you're not too good at it.'

Shifty Fly glared at him. He had had a right dressing down from Eddie Ferrantino for letting Angelo give him the slip.

'Don't hang around on my account,' Angelo continued, 'I'm not going anywhere.' he leaned back in his seat and closed his eyes. He hoped that by the time he opened them Shifty Fly would be gone. He was.

The day had been a fuck up. Screaming in every direction. Enzio from New York. Eddie

Ferrantino in London. Christ knows what he was supposed to have done. Free, white, and over twenty-one, he had shacked up with a chick and not told anyone where he was. Terrible thing. A crime.

'Would you like to order a drink, sir?' asked the hostess. She was pretty in a plastic, groomed sort of way.

Normally he would have imagined screwing her, but his head was so full of other things he hardly noticed her. 'Just a coke,' he said.

The two seats beside him were empty, and he was pleased about that. Later he would be able to lie out and have a sleep.

He was nervous about seeing his father. His father was going to scream about the way he looked. He hadn't even had time to get his hair trimmed and it was now as long and thick as a rock superstar's.

He wished he could tell Enzio Bassalino to go fuck himself. But he couldn't. He knew he couldn't. Yet he didn't know why he couldn't.

The big jet was taxiing down the runway and Angelo allowed himself to think about Rio. She was a hell of a woman, the sort of woman who would stand up to someone like Enzio. He admired her. She was terrific. She did her own thing.

Then again she was a sadistic bitch. And he wasn't happy about her hyping his drink with something he didn't know about.

He wondered if she would call him. His fast

departure for New York would surprise her, maybe she would think he was running away. From what? He had nothing to run away from. So some guy had made it with him. Big deal. So what. Most men had at least one homosexual experience in their lives.

But when he thought about it his skin began to crawl, his stomach to churn, a helpless excitement crept through his body and he knew, although he wouldn't admit it, that it was something he would want to try again.

Lara went to Kennedy Airport to meet Prince Alfa Masserini. She had called him and told him she needed him, and although in the middle of a backgammon tournament in Gstaad he had promised to fly at once to her side.

She had decided to meet his plane because she had to keep occupied. She had to try and immerse herself in the world she knew. She had been doing too much thinking and it wasn't good. It lined your skin, and ruined your sleep and gave you a guilt complex about spending thousands of dollars on clothes when people were starving in the world. Prince Alfa should be able to pull her back into a state of immersion. Prince Alfa was good at that.

At the airport she bumped straight into Nick.

They stared at each other for a moment of surprise, then Lara smiled the hurt out of her eyes and extended a hand for her customary

European handshake. 'Are you returning to Los Angeles?' she enquired politely.

'No,' Nick shook his head, 'my brother's coming in from London, I'm meeting him. And you?'

'A friend from Europe, I'm meeting them.' She didn't know why she said them. Why hadn't she said my fiancé, Prince Alfa Masserini, a Roman Prince, not a miserable half-breed Yankee Italian like you.

Twenty-four hours previously they had been in bed together. Now they stood like nervous strangers, Nick peering at his watch, Lara glancing around in the faint hope that she might bump into someone else she knew.

'I guess I'd better check on the flight, see it's on time,' Nick said. 'What flight are you meeting? Give me the number and I'll check that too.'

She handed him a piece of paper where she had scribbled details.

'Wait here,' he commanded.

As soon as he'd gone she had an insane desire to run. How childish. She wrapped her lynx coat tightly round her and stood her ground.

He returned shortly. She noticed women watching him. He was the sort of man you looked at twice. You almost recognised him. Was he an actor, a singer?

'We're meeting the same plane,' he announced, 'delayed two hours. Want to go to the airport motel and make mad, incredible love?' He was smiling slightly. A joke?

She smiled back, coldly. 'I don't think so.'

'Pity,' Nick was in control, 'you look very beautiful, like you've done very beautiful things lately.'

'How's April?'

'Fine,' Nick lied, 'everything's fine. She understands it was just a bit of gossip.'

'But it wasn't.'

Nick laughed uneasily. 'Yeah, sure. You know that, and *I* know that, but *we* aren't telling, are we?'

Lara enjoyed the moment. 'Aren't we?'

Nick gripped her firmly by the arm. 'I'm going to buy you a drink,' he announced, 'we can't just stand around here for two hours.'

'I'm going back to the city, I've decided not to wait.'

'Then you've got time for a drink first.'

She wanted to say no, turn and run, get out of his life. But her body wanted to stay next to his, and her body wouldn't move.

He led her to a bar and sat her in a corner booth. She ordered champagne and orange juice, and the cocktail waitress looked at her as if she was some kind of nut.

'I probably won't be able to get back to the Coast for a couple more days,' Nick remarked, 'so if you're going to be around maybe we could ...'

'Maybe we could what?' Lara interrupted

angrily. 'Have a few more secret interludes? A little bit of fun on the side that April won't find out about?'

'You didn't object yesterday.'

'Yesterday I didn't know you were going to turn to jelly as soon as you saw our names together in a newspaper.'

'You *know* the scene with April and me. I haven't been keeping secrets. But that doesn't change the way you turn me on, you know you turn me on. And it's the same for you, isn't it?' He took hold of her hand in his and held it tightly. 'We've got vibes together, so don't fight it.'

How easy to agree with him. Two or three more days of incredible sex.

'You meet your friends,' he was saying, 'I'll meet my brother, we'll get all that over with, and then later I can come by your apartment. Nobody need know, only you and I. That way we're all winners. Have you got a spare key?'

Revenge was sweet. 'Yes, I have,' Lara said, fumbling in her purse. 'You know, I think that's a very good idea, Nick.'

Chapter 33

It wasn't fair to blame Beth, Frank reasoned. It wasn't her fault that Anna Maria had caught them together. She was a good kid, genuinely sweet and concerned. He regretted his phone call telling her to get out. That had been a stupid thing to do. He needed her now, and the children needed her. How many girls like Beth were there around? Not many, he could vouch for that. The day of the innocent girl was over. They were all little grafters and hustlers out for what they could get.

He wanted her back. But how to get hold of her?

He couldn't remember which employment agency had sent her, so all of them were checked, but none of them seemed to know her.

He remembered her interview and the references she had brought with her. References that he hadn't even bothered to check, because he had liked her at first glance and could see she was honest. He found himself in the frustrating position of not knowing where she was, or any more about her than the fact that her name was Beth.

He put people on the job of finding her, she would probably check into the agencies looking for a new job. Meanwhile, because of his own stupidity, he could only sit and wait. And sitting and waiting meant thinking, and he did not like the thoughts that crowded his head. So he drank, and drinking meant a sweet oblivion that only hit him after a full bottle of Scotch, and being drunk meant he couldn't work.

Enzio gave strict instructions to Segal and Golli not to let him out of their sight, and to keep him at home. There would be time enough after the funeral to pull Frank back into shape, meanwhile Enzio took over.

He met with an old friend, Stefano Crown. He was sympathetic, he too was having troubles with the new, mainly black, groups that were trying to muscle in.

'What's the solution?' Enzio asked.

Stefano Crown shrugged. He was younger than Enzio by fifteen years, and still kept complete control of his 'business' interests. 'I'll bargain with them,' he said, 'probably give them a piece of action, bring some of them in.'

Enzio spat his disgust on the floor. He had had trouble with Stefano Crown before. 'You give them some, they want more; you give them more, they want all.'

'I run legitimate businesses,' Stefano said. 'Last week they blew up two of my supermarkets. I can't have that. I can't have the ordinary people who work for me too frightened to drag their asses in in the mornings. Last week thirty-three employees quit—*thirty-three*. Word gets around. Soon I'll have them all running, then what will I do when there is no one to work in the beauty parlours, garages, supermarkets, what then?'

Enzio spat again. All Stefano was concerned about was his legitimate front. Things were so different from the old days. 'You go with them, you get no help from me,' Enzio said, 'I have other plans, better plans.'

Stefano shook his head. 'I don't want any more trouble. I pay my taxes. I'm a businessman now. What does Frank want?'

'Frank,' Enzio sighed. 'Frank has other things on his mind. You heard about Anna Maria?'

Stefano nodded. 'Terrible tragedy.'

'The funeral's tomorrow. It would be a sign of respect if you were to attend.'

'Of course. Of course. No hard feelings, Enzio?'

'Not at all.'

* * *

Later that day Stefano Crown was shot in the head as he was about to enter an apartment building on Riverside Drive.

'It's a terrible thing when a man can no longer move freely in this city,' Enzio said with feeling when he heard.

Alio Marcusi, who was with him at the time, merely smiled.

Chapter 34

'Hey Angelo baby, you're looking good, really good.'

Angelo and Nick hugged, smiled. They were genuinely pleased to see each other.

Angelo scratched his beard ruefully. 'I guess the old man's going to pop a few buttons when he sees this.'

'Well, you are a bit hairy,' Nick admitted, 'but nothing that a good barber couldn't take care of.'

'Forget it,' Angelo said quickly, 'I like it, it stays.'

'Sure,' Nick agreed. 'I'm not the one that has to kiss you.'

Angelo looked at him sharply. Was there a snide meaning to that remark?

'How was the flight?' Nick enquired, 'pretty hostesses? Word filters back that you were quite a stud in London, but then you always were a horny little bastard. Hey, remember that time you were shacking up with the little starlet and her boyfriend beat the pants off you?'

'Yeah.'

'Trouble with you is you were always getting caught. A boyfriend here, a husband there.'

Angelo nodded.

'Come on, let's get moving, Enzio's waiting to see you. By the way, take no notice of the armed escort, Enzio's got some crazy idea that we make good targets.'

Angelo glanced around and noticed two men close by. They followed Angelo and Nick to the car and got in the front.

Nick took no notice of them, but Angelo couldn't help feeling uncomfortable. He preferred Shifty Fly to a couple of anonymous hoods who looked ready to pump a bullet into anyone.

'What the hell's going on?' Angelo questioned, as soon as they were in the car. 'Why was I dragged back here so fast?'

Nick stared out of the window, 'You heard about Anna Maria?'

'No, what? She had the baby?'

'She's dead, kid. She fell down the stairs at the house.'

'Fell down the stairs? How could that happen, was she sick?'

Nick shrugged.

'Hey, did Frank beat up on her. Did that lousy shit . . .'

Nick shook his head warningly at the men in the front seat. 'We'll talk about it later,' he said.

'Jesus!' Angelo exclaimed, 'I always liked Anna Maria, she wasn't bad at all . . . Jesus, Nick, it's really terrible.'

Enzio waited at Frank's house. Frank was in the kitchen nursing a bottle of Scotch, Golli and Segal close by.

Enzio waited with Alio in the living-room. Two of his men were near the back door, two at the front, and a further two were sitting in separate parked cars outside.

You couldn't be too careful. Especially now, with Stefano Crown's son bent on revenge. He seemed to think that Enzio was responsible for his father's death.

'Nothing to do with me,' Enzio proclaimed, hurt and angry that Georgio Crown should even suspect him. 'It was those mad black bastards. Those pieces of shit Stefano wanted to go partners with.'

Georgio Crown did not believe him. The Crowns had already opened negotiations with certain black groups, and it would not be to their advantage to put a bullet in Stefano Crown. In fact, it was to their disadvantage.

'I think Georgio Crown should be the next to go,' Enzio remarked mildly to Alio. 'Arrange it. Oh, and also my friend, please see that a wreath is sent to Stefano's funeral on behalf of myself and family.'

Enzio felt better than he had felt in years. Life in New York was most exhilarating. Miami had been getting rather boring for a man who had always lived such an active life. Fuck all the Bassalino rivals.

Enzio was giving them a taste of their own medicine.

After her drink with Nick, Lara returned to the city.

She was confused, filled with mixed emotions, and furious with herself for having got mixed up in the whole bizarre business.

She phoned Cass.

'Count me out,' she said, 'I'm sorry but I've had enough.'

'I was trying to call you,' Cass replied. 'I've seen Dukey. He wants to work it out his way. He wants you all out, and I think he's right.'

Lara wasn't really listening. 'I just don't want to be involved any more. What we are doing is crazy.'

'Right,' Cass agreed. 'Crazy. Now I've got to find Rio. I don't know exactly what Dukey has planned, but whatever it is I don't think it's too safe to be around the Bassalinos.'

'She'll probably be in New York. Nick was

meeting Angelo at the airport. Cass, I think I'm going back to Europe,' she laughed bitterly, 'back to the old high life. Fun and games amongst the jet set. Look, I'll keep in touch. Give my love to Beth if you see her.' She hung up.

So what good had it all done? Nick appeared to be as resilient as ever. Were they all supposed to be glad that Frank Bassalino's wife was dead along with his unborn child?

Lara studied her face in the bathroom mirror. She seemed to look different, only she didn't know why. Ugly, I look ugly she thought. Carefully she took off all her make-up, then just as carefully she started to apply fresh make-up. She did it three times before she was satisfied. Then she sat in a chair staring at the front door and waiting for Prince Alfa.

'You little punk!' Enzio spat, clapping Angelo round the shoulders, kissing him on both cheeks, 'look at you, you look like a fuckin' communist!'

Angelo joined in the laughter that followed. His father had been saying that to him for years now.

'Good to be home, huh?' Enzio said. 'Good to be with the family in times of trouble.'

'Yeah, sure,' Angelo agreed half-heartedly. If there was any trouble he wanted to be long gone.

'You seen your other brother yet? Go to him, pay your respects.'

'Yes, Enzio.'

Nick went with Angelo to find Frank, he was sprawled half asleep in the kitchen.

Angelo said, 'Hey, Frank, I'm sorry 'bout things.'

Frank grunted.

'Shit, this house is depressing,' Angelo muttered to Nick, 'I hope I'm not supposed to be staying here.'

'No, you're at the hotel with Enzio. Anna Maria's mother and sister are arriving later, they're staying here.'

'How long does the old man expect me to hang around?'

Nick shrugged. 'I don't know. The funeral's tomorrow, then Enzio has some half-assed idea that we go with him to Miami for the weekend, see Rose. I think there's trouble planned for the weekend, and he wants us out of New York. Personally I just want to get back to the Coast.'

Angelo scratched his beard. 'Don't you sometimes wish you were born an orphan?'

Chapter 35

'You look wonderful,' Prince Alfa Masserini said, kissing Lara on both cheeks, 'you have not changed, still the most beautiful.'

'It's only been a few months.'

'A few months too long. I have missed you. You have made me look foolish to my friends. All the time they tease me, make jokes. Lara has left, they all say. Your family business has taken you far too long.'

'I'm sorry,' Lara said quietly.

'It is good you are sorry,' the Prince said, loosening his tie, and examining his face in a wall mirror for the wearisome signs of travel. 'I think now you will not run off like that again.'

'No, I won't,' Lara agreed. 'It was important

at the time, but now . . .' she shrugged. 'Are you hungry? I could fix you some bacon and eggs.'

'Shall we not dine out?'

'I thought we would stay in,' she moved close to him, 'it's been so long.'

Later in bed Prince Alfa slept, and Lara lay awake beside him. He was a good lover, accomplished, considerate.

He did nothing for her. He made her feel empty, used. With Nick it had been so different. So right.

She wondered if Nick was going to turn up. She glanced at the bedside clock, it was late, and she hoped that he wouldn't come. It had been stupid of her to give him her key. Such a petty form of revenge.

She wished Prince Alfa did not have such an offensive snore. It was very annoying, it was keeping her awake.

Later she did sleep fitfully, and she did not know Nick was in the apartment until he switched the bedroom light on and pulled the bedclothes roughly off her and Alfa. She awoke all groggy and managed a smile. 'Hello, Nick.'

Outraged, Prince Alfa demanded, 'Who is this person?' as he reached for his pure silk underpants.

'You really win the prize,' Nick said, shaking his head and staring down at her, 'Jesus Christ, you really do.'

She didn't try to cover herself. She just stared back at him.

Prince Alfa flung on a paisley dressing-gown. 'What do you want?' he said, his voice becoming high-pitched and out of control.

'There's nothing I want here,' Nick said, throwing the door key so it landed on her body. 'Nothing worth having. Nothing even worth paying for!'

'Cover yourself,' Prince Alfa shrieked at Lara.

'I've seen it all before,' Nick said coldly, 'every quivering high-class-hooker inch of it.'

'I don't understand . . .' Prince Alfa whined.

'Nor do I, buddy boy, nor do I.' Nick turned abruptly to leave, but Prince Alfa grabbed him by the sleeve. Nick shook himself free. 'Have you slept with her?'

'Run away, ponce, before I lose my temper,' Nick said slowly.

'You will answer my question!'

With a supple, easy movement Nick smashed his knee into Prince Alfa's groin, at the same time his fist connected with the Prince's jaw. The Prince collapsed in a huddle on the floor.

Lara lay perfectly still. Nick paused and glanced at her. He went to speak, thought better of it, and left.

Frank couldn't sleep. He refused to go to bed. He sat in a chair in the kitchen guzzling on a bottle of Scotch and occasionally dozing. It had been that way ever since the accident . . .

Nobody said anything to him, they left him alone. Enzio had attempted to engage him in conversation about business activities, but after a while he had given up. 'After the funeral you'll pull yourself together,' Enzio had muttered, 'a few days in Miami. You'll see your mother.'

Like hell he would go to Miami. He wasn't going anywhere until they found Beth.

Anna Maria's mother and sister arrived. It was fortunate they did not speak English. After a short greeting they left him alone, and that was the way he wanted it. Alone with his thoughts, his ideas for the future. Family business activities did not enter his mind at all, let Enzio worry about that.

He thought he might take a vacation, go to Hawaii, or Acapulco. Somewhere far, somewhere he could be alone with Beth.

After the funeral he would find her, he had no doubt of that.

Nick left Lara's apartment in a fury. How could she have done a thing like that to him?

He went to the best whorehouse in New York. *Something* had to calm him down.

They put out the red carpet for him.

Nick Bassalino. Enzio's son, Frank's brother. It was almost like a visit from royalty.

The madame herself, a Scandinavian lady,

with big boobs and a girlish face, had offered to serve him personally. He had declined her invitation and chosen instead a sour-faced redhead who had kept the whole project on the impersonal level he wished for.

Afterwards he was so pissed off at the whole scene that he got good and truly bombed on straight brandy.

Finally he had gone back to his hotel, slept fitfully, and placed a call to April Crawford in Los Angeles for early morning.

The call came through whilst he was still asleep, and he held the phone to his ear and listened to the long distance ringing while he tried to open his eyes. His mouth felt like lead shit.

Faithful Hattie told the operator Miss Crawford was not at home, so he spoke to Hattie.

'Hey, Hat, what's happening? She *still* mad?'

'Haven't you heard, Mr Bassalino?' Hattie sounded embarrassed.

'Heard what?'

'Miss Crawford and Mr Albert got married yesterday.'

Nick was silent.

'Mr Bassalino, you there?' Hattie enquired, her voice worried. 'I told Miss Crawford she should have called you.'

Nick hung up the phone. He was white. He called down to the desk and had them send up the newspapers, and there it was in black and white.

April Crawford and Sammy Albert.
Las Vegas. Monday.
April Crawford took husband number five
today in a quiet ceremony in the garden
of Stanley Graham's 'Hi-style' Hotel.
Sammy Albert, thirty-year-old star of
Road Job, Tiger and *Prince California* was
the lucky man. His only comment on the
twenty-year age difference, was, 'April is a
real lady, a class lady, her age is of no
interest to me.'

Nick threw the paper on the floor in disgust.
Jesus Christ but April was stupid. Any woman
who could marry a juvenile super-stud like
Sammy Albert was stupid. April must have
done it in a fit of jealous rage.

Nick felt more disappointed than anything
else. Disappointed in April. She was a grown
woman, she knew what she was doing.

In a strange way he also felt relieved. Now
that he didn't have to answer to April he was
free. And now that he was free he could do
something about Lara . . .

Chapter 36

Leroy Jesus Bauls did not smoke, it was bad for your health, and Leroy never did anything that was bad for his health.

He was still at a loss to explain his behaviour at *Manny's*. What a stupid fucked-up thing to have done, getting the old lady and the kid out. So it had turned out all right, and that was lucky. But it had meant taking unnecessary risks, and that was not his bag.

Never again, he vowed. If anyone got in his way in the future that was their problem.

Once again he wore his errand boy clothes as he sat in the parked van a block away from the entrance to the cemetery. A lesson Leroy had learned early in life was that a black in New York could hang around anywhere as long as he was dressed for the part. Wear something sharp and stand on a street corner and the fuzz were soon at your elbow hustling you, moving you on. Stand there like a janitor holding a broom, and you were on your own, nobody noticed you.

Leroy was parked in a prime position to watch the limousines as they arrived in a long, dark, sober parade. His shades were fitted with special telescopic sights so recognising the mourners was no problem.

He noted that Enzio Bassalino was taking no chances. He was surrounded by his men, old men in shiny suits with nervous, darting hands.

Nick and Angelo arrived in a car together, they too were surrounded. They waited on the pavement for the mother and sister who came in the next car.

Leroy sat perfectly still, watching, noting every detail.

He was good at waiting, the first words he could remember being spoken to him when he was a kid were, 'You sit still and wait. Y'hear me? Just wait.' His mother repeated that phrase to him every day as she left him outside hotel rooms. It was only when he got big enough to peek through keyholes that he real- ised why she wanted him to wait.

Frank Bassalino arrived, and Leroy's knuck- les slowly whitened as he gripped the steering wheel hard. It was the only sign he gave that Frank was the one he had been waiting for.

Eventually they all disappeared into the cemetery, the family, relatives, and friends. A group of four men remained outside. They split into twos, and stayed at each side of the gates, their eyes watchful.

Leroy did not move for ten minutes, then he got out of the van, opened up the back and took out a giant wreath. He carried it slowly down the street towards the cemetery.

'Yeah? Whacha want?' One of the men blocked his path at the gate.

'Special delivery for the Bassalino funeral.'

'Leave it here.'

'Sure,' Leroy deposited the wreath on the ground and fumbled in his pocket for the receipt book. 'Sign here, please.'

The man scrawled an illegible signature. Leroy hesitated, as if waiting for a tip. 'You want me to take it through?' he questioned. 'I was told it had to be left by the grave.'

'Just leave it.'

Leroy shrugged. 'It's your funeral,' he muttered to himself as he walked back to the van.

Exactly eight minutes later the four men standing by the cemetery gates were blown to pieces. Leroy, now parked three blocks away, heard the explosion clearly. He waited half a minute and then walked slowly back to view the chaos.

He was carrying a brown paper parcel. Police sirens screamed through the air, a crowd was gathering. Leroy found it an easy job to place the package he was carrying on the front seat of the limousine Frank Bassalino had arrived in. The chauffeur had left the car and was amongst the crowd by the cemetery gates. The line of parked limousines was deserted. If he had wanted to he could have left a package in each car. But that wasn't the way Dukey K. Williams wanted it.

Within minutes Enzio and his sons came hurrying out. There was much confusion, women weeping, the crowd growing by the minute.

Leroy strolled off casually.

Chapter 37

Angelo could feel the fear in his stomach, his throat was dry, his skin pallid.

They had been standing by the grave when the explosion had sounded. Instinctively he had dropped to the ground, burying his head in his hands. Jesus, what a noise! What was he doing here anyway in this maniac city when he should be in London.

Nick had dragged him up. 'Stay easy,' he had warned, 'don't panic.'

Enzio had already sent people to find out what had happened. Within minutes they were back. A bomb.

Enzio took command. 'Go to the cars, eyes open, stay in groups. Golli, Segal, hold on to Frank.'

Frank appeared to be unaffected by the explosion. He had started the day drunk, and with the help of a flask in his pocket he planned to end the day drunk.

'Go straight to the airport,' Enzio instructed, '*don't* stop by Frank's house or the hotel.'

No one argued. With bombs going off around them a weekend in Miami seemed like a good idea.

'I'll go with Frank,' Nick said.

'No, stay with Angelo,' Enzio commanded, noticing how white-faced and shaky his younger son was.

Nick didn't argue. He just wanted to get the fuck out of there before the police arrived. Let Enzio deal with the police, he was the one with enough connections to wire a building.

They bundled into the cars.

'Those guys,' Angelo mumbled, 'those poor guys . . .'

'Just thank your skinny balls it wasn't you,' Nick said, 'it was probably meant to be.'

'Me?' Angelo was incredulous, 'why me?'

'You, me, Frank. What difference, we're all Bassalinos.'

Angelo nodded helplessly, yes, they were all Bassalinos and that meant anyone having a rumble with old Enzio automatically included his three sons.

'Who do you think did . . . ?'

'Listen kid, I don't want to talk. Just sit back

and relax, turn on or something, but just leave me alone, I've got to think.'

Nick closed his eyes. He had been trying to get his thoughts straight all day. It wasn't easy, for someone who didn't drink he had one hell of a hangover. The business with Lara had really turned him over. Jesus, she had planned it, *wanted* him to find her in bed with that Italian ponce.

What a bitch. What a prize bitch.

He hoped he had damaged the guy.

He wished he had damaged her.

And as for April Crawford it was a joke. She and Sammy Albert together were a bad joke.

'I don't know why I couldn't have stayed in London,' Angelo complained, interrupting Nick's thoughts.

Before Nick could reply they both heard the explosion. It came from behind.

The car with Frank in it was behind.

Chapter 38

Prince Alfa Masserini had a broken nose. 'I will sue that man for every penny he's got,' he ranted from his private clinic bed, his perfect Roman nose encased in a plaster cast.

'You don't know who he is,' Lara remarked calmly.

Prince Alfa swore in Italian, then, 'Lara, you are being very stupid, a very stupid girl. I thought perhaps there was a future together for us, but now . . .' he shrugged.

Lara got up from the chair beside the bed and nodded, 'You're right Alfa, you really are right.'

'Where are you going?'

Lara shook her head. 'I don't know. Maybe Paris, maybe Acapulco.'

'You wait a few days,' Alfa said confidentially, 'I will forgive you. We will go somewhere together.'

'I don't want to be forgiven,' Lara said slowly, 'I'm not a little child, I'm sorry about your nose. I'm sorry about everything. I just think it's best that we don't see each other again.'

'Lara!' the Prince was shocked. 'What do you mean? I have waited these last months, I have made certain plans for us. My mother, she looks forward to meeting you. We will ski first, then on to Rome where I will present you to my family.'

'No,' Lara interrupted, 'it's over.' She walked from the room as he burst into a monologue of angry Italian.

She felt completely blank. Nothing mattered, nothing mattered at all. She was very tired, and the only thought that appealed to her was to get into bed and sleep. She wished the impossible. She wished she had Margaret to talk to.

Outside she climbed into the chauffeured car and closed her eyes. 'Back to my apartment,' she told the driver.

'City's goin' mad,' the driver informed her, 'hoodlums runnin' wild blowin' each other up. It ain't even safe drivin' no more.'

Lara wasn't really listening. She was already drifting into sleep.

* * *

There was no body to identify. No body to bury. Frank Bassalino had been blown into a thousand little pieces. Two people innocently standing near the car were killed, many more injured as the blast blew out all the windows in nearby office buildings and glass came showering down.

Nick didn't hang around. He took it all in at a glance and he knew Frank had no chance. He hauled Angelo out of their car, and holding him tightly by the arm, walked him away from the wreckage.

Angelo was too shaken to talk. Nick moved quickly and they were three blocks away when the police cars, sirens screaming, came rushing past.

When he was sure that they weren't being followed, Nick hailed a cab and told the driver to go to the airport.

'Somebody's going to get his balls sledge-hammered for this,' Nick said at last, 'and I am going to do it. I am going to cut his balls off and string them up for salami.'

'Who . . .?' Angelo asked.

'We'll find out. We always find out. Nobody gets away with killing a Bassalino.'

'You sound like Enzio.'

'I hope so, little brother, I really hope so.'

* * *

Rio Java flew into New York and saw the headlines.

She went straight to Cass's apartment. Dukey was there. 'You arranged it?' she asked.

He shrugged. 'Maybe, maybe not. We're not the only ones who want to see the Bassalinos go down.'

'Well, don't touch Angelo, he's mine. Understand, brother?'

'Sure,' Dukey agreed, 'if you get him first.'

'I don't want to get him, I just want to destroy him. Wasn't that supposed to be the plan?'

Dukey nodded. 'That was before. Things are different now.'

'What do you mean things are different now?'

'Let's just call it a little racial problem, and leave it at that.'

'Racial problem my ass!' Rio exclaimed.

'Listen, girl, you had your chance. You blew it. Now it's my turn.'

'Oh,' said Rio coldly, 'you mean I'm supposed to drop everything on account of what *you* say.'

'Clever girl.'

'Beth and Lara are out,' Cass said quickly, 'I think Dukey's right, Rio.'

Rio turned on her quickly, 'Well fuck you, too.'

Dukey's eyes were hard and cold. 'Shame you're not black.'

'I'm multi-coloured, it's more fun.'

'You're just pissed off that you can't have any more of your little games.'

'I can do what I like.'

Dukey nodded in agreement. 'Only don't do it near the Bassalinos, otherwise your long, skinny, multi-coloured ass is going to join them in hell.'

Chapter 39

Mary Ann August smiled at Claire and Claire said, 'Honey, you've really surprised me, things are working out fine. Mr Forbes was very pleased today and for Mr Forbes to be pleased—well, that's really something.'

'He promised he would be back soon,' Mary Ann said, stretching her arms up so that the short, white nightdress she was wearing pulled up and exposed a fine matting of pale coffee-coloured pubic hair.

Claire's eyes wandered down to take a look and she bit on her lip nervously. No problems with this one. Some girls were just born to be whores.

Mary Ann flopped back on the bed and her thighs parted. 'Gee, Claire, I wish I could take a walk, I'm really cheesed about being shut in all the time.'

'Next week.'

Mary Ann pouted. 'You can trust me, I'm not gonna run off. I *like* it here. I like you . . .'

Claire moved nearer the bed. 'You're a smart girl, you're no trouble. A girl like you can make a lot of money. Now that we've fixed your hair, you look so pretty.'

Mary Ann smiled. 'Enzio wouldn't like it.'

Claire sat down on the bed, and casually ran her fingers along Mary Ann's leg. 'Enzio's not going to have to like it, is he?'

Mary Ann giggled and spread her legs apart. 'Are you a dyke, Claire?' she asked innocently.

The pressure of Claire's fingers hardened. 'I've seen too many pot bellies and limp hard-ons to be anything else,' she paused. 'Did you ever try it?'

Mary Ann giggled again. 'Mr Forbes didn't make me come,' her eyes widened, 'I told him a little head would do the trick but Mr Forbes said that was *my* job.'

Claire bent slowly down, her eyes bright, 'Mr Forbes must be screwy in the mind.'

Mary Ann sighed and lay back to enjoy the administrations of Claire. Five minutes passed, and then carefully Mary Ann reached under the bed and gripped the chair leg she had put there earlier.

She raised her body slowly, until only the top of Claire's close-cropped hair was visible. She moaned, and Claire's efforts increased. Then slowly, so as not to disturb anything, Mary Ann raised the chair leg and smashed it down heavily on Claire's head. Once, twice, three times.

There was blood as Claire slumped to the floor, and Mary Ann was sorry about that. But Mary Ann had no intention of being locked up and forced into the life of a hooker. Oh no. Oh dear me, no. Not Mary Ann August. Not after she had worked hard and put up with Enzio Bassalino for all those months. She had a Chinchilla coat, jewellery, clothes, a mink coat. She had possessions that were worth money, enough money that if she sold them she could go back to the little town in Texas she hailed from, and buy herself a very nice little business. A boutique or a beauty parlour. She had known her time with Enzio was not a permanent thing, and she had planned accordingly.

She dressed quickly and took money and keys from Claire's pocketbook.

She had possessions, and sonofabitch she was going to get them.

Chapter 40

By the next day the house in Miami was buzzing with activity. There was a meeting in progress.

Enzio sat behind his desk, his eyes were red-rimmed and his shoulders slumped heavily. Beside him stood Nick, doing most of the talking, words coming hard and fast.

Enzio appeared to have aged ten years, he listened to his middle son, occasionally nodding to let the room crowded with men know that he was in agreement with everything Nick said.

Angelo hunched in a chair nearby. He was scared, and it showed in his white face and the shaking of his hand as he sipped mouthfuls of Scotch from a large tumbler. What he really wanted was to get good and truly stoned, a few joints might calm him down and stop the shaking. Only he couldn't do that in front of Enzio. Enzio didn't approve.

Nick was surprisingly cool. He issued instructions. He wanted information and he wanted it fast. 'I want to know before the end of the day who is responsible. Five thousand dollars for the right information.'

The meeting was over and the men dispersed.

'Rose . . .' mumbled Enzio, 'somebody's got to tell Rose.'

Angelo buried himself in his drink. Rose scared the shit out of him. She always had.

'I'll tell her,' said Nick. He had always been able to cope with Rose better than the others. He would joke and laugh with her, and sometimes he would be able to summon up a faint smile from her otherwise dead face. 'I'll go see her now.'

Rose was sitting at her chair by the window.

Nick crept up and squeezed her from behind. 'Ciao, Mama!' He was shocked at how thin she had suddenly become.

She looked up at him and nodded slightly.

'Sorry it's been so long, Mama, but I've been busy out on the Coast. You look fine, really fine.'

Nick could remember his mother before she had locked herself away. He could remember

222

her startling beauty, and vivacious personality, and the way she could make friends so easily.

He could also remember the night it all happened. He had been about sixteen and out on a date, and when he had returned home Alio had met him at the door and told him his mother was sick. 'You're to stay at my house tonight,' Alio had said, 'Angelo and the nanny are already there.'

Alio hadn't even let him into the house to fetch some clothes. He had bundled him back into his car and told him to go. He wasn't allowed home for two weeks, and when he was he found his mother had locked herself away and she never emerged from the room again.

'Frank's dead,' Nick said, 'it was an ... accident.'

Rose spun round and stared at him. She still had the most magnificent eyes he had ever seen. They could burn a hole in you, they were so deep and bright and strong. Her eyes spoke for her, they wanted him to tell her more.

'It was an accident, in a car,' Nick put his arms round her. What more could he say?

Chapter 41

'Strike, before they can strike back.' Those were the orders Leroy Jesus Bauls received from Dukey K. Williams.

Which was why he was now on the road to Miami. It was a long drive, but it would have been too dangerous to fly with the equipment he needed to travel with. All the fuss there was at airports today, luggage being searched and people being frisked. He wouldn't have got anywhere near a plane.

His black Mercedes flew down the highway at a steady pace. He felt completely at ease, his mind clear and able to deal with the plans he had formed.

He had inspected Enzio Bassalino's mansion a few days previously. With Enzio in New York the grounds had not been so closely guarded and Leroy had been able to set things up exactly as he wanted them.

He was well aware of the guards at the gates, the alarm systems, the dogs.

It was an exciting job, a challenge, and Leroy enjoyed challenges.

Mary Ann August bought a black wig. It was long and covered her blondeness nicely. She bought blue denims, a T-shirt, a man's shirt and tinted glasses. She took off her make-up in the Ladies' Room at the store where she had made her purchases and when she emerged she looked like a different girl.

She took a cab to the airport and bought a ticket for Miami.

She was very nervous. There had been a lot of money in Claire's purse and they would come after her if just for that. But they wouldn't find her—she didn't even recognise herself in the mirror.

She bought some magazines and boarded the plane.

Nick was in charge. The old man had gone to pieces, his age suddenly and surprisingly catching up with him.

Angelo sat around, jumpy as a cat, and Nick finally got one of the boys to fix him up with a couple of joints to calm him down.

After the meeting Nick phoned Los Angeles to check on his business there. Everything seemed OK. He had good people working there, people he could trust.

Lara's face kept wandering around in his thoughts, funnily enough he had forgotten about April. So he wasn't going to be Mr. April Crawford. Big Deal. So what! In a way he was relieved.

The old man was having a sleep and Angelo was playing cards out by the pool.

Nick called the gate. No problems. He had put an extra man out there, three of them on constant alert, and no one was allowed through unless they got Nick's personal OK.

The Bassalino family was under fire, and Nick was taking no risks.

He picked up the phone and dialled Lara's number in New York.

She took her time to answer and then mumbled, 'Hello?'

'I should have killed him,' Nick said slowly. She didn't answer, so he added, 'If I catch anybody in bed with you again I will kill them.'

'You broke his nose.'

'Did I? Did I really?'

Lara started to cry. She was so pleased to hear from him, so ridiculously pleased.

'Go to the airport,' Nick was saying, 'get on the next flight to Miami, you should just make the two o'clock. There will be a guy called Mario to meet you, he'll bring you straight to the house.'

'I can't, Nick, I . . .'

'No arguments, sweetheart, we'll argue when you get here. I really need you here, I really need you . . .'

When Lara hung up she was laughing and crying at the same time.

He *needed* her. He *wanted* her.

She started to pack a few things, humming softly to herself.

Then suddenly Cass's words hit her. Words that she hadn't really listened to before were very clear in her head.

'I don't know exactly what Dukey has planned, but I don't think it's safe to be around the Bassalinos. He wants you all out and I think he's right.'

Lara felt a moment of panic.

She phoned Cass quickly. 'What did you mean?' she asked. 'What does Dukey plan to do?'

'I don't know,' Cass said, 'I guess he's going to finish off . . .'

'Finish off what?'

'I don't know.'

Lara hung up and dialled Dukey's number. There was no reply.

She had to get to Nick, tell him the truth, warn him.

She finished her packing in a few minutes and sent the doorman to get her a cab.

She had to get to Miami as quickly as possible. There was no other way of warning him.

In her room Rose Bassalino brooded. She had no tears left to cry for her eldest son. Her tears had all been used many years before

It was Enzio's fault of course. Everything was always Enzio's fault.

He had taken away Frank because he knew that Frank was her favourite son.

If she closed her eyes she could see in vivid detail the scene of that night so many years ago when Enzio and his 'assistants' had sliced Charles Cardwell to death. Like a piece of beef they had chopped and sliced and hacked.

And Enzio had held her, his hand on her breasts, his body stiffening with excitement.

Rose stifled a scream as the memories crowded back. She went to her window and stared out. The pool was still there, the grass, the trees. She had trained her mind to go blank, shut out everything, concentrate on the scenery.

Today it didn't work. Today the sun-drenched garden and mosaic-tiled swimming pool did nothing to calm her.

She was not mad. She knew she was not mad. But to hang on to her sanity she had shut herself away, and now she could feel the fury building up in her body, a fury that was giving her new strength.

She had shut herself away for her children's sake, to spare them the agony of what she might do. Now it didn't matter. Frank was gone. Enzio had planned it.

Rose stepped away from the window. She knew what she had to do. Her mind was clear for the first time in years.

Chapter 42

'Angelo—telephone,' Alio strolled out to the pool to tell him.

'For me?'

'Yeah—a woman.' Alio was not interested.

Angelo put down his cards. Nobody knew where he was. He picked up the phone beside the pool.

'You little prick,' a familiar voice said, 'running away ain't gonna get you but nowhere, baby!'

'Rio, you bum. How did you find me?'

'I smelt you out, baby,' she laughed, 'we still friends?'

Angelo relaxed for the first time in days. 'Yeah, but I want to talk to you.'

'To me,' she paused, '*and* my friends.'

'Listen, that was strictly a one-time scene.'

'Sure, sure. And you hated it—right?'

Angelo felt the tingles of excitement that he had felt that time in Rio's flat. 'I don't go that route,' he said slowly.

'Oh, *come on*,' Rio replied mockingly, 'this is *me* you're talking to. And I am right here at the Fontainebleu with two divine friends who are *aching* to meet you. Shall we come to you, or will you sashay your *nice* tight ass over here?'

Angelo's throat was dry, his clothes felt too tight and hot.

'I can't see you today,' he said weakly. Nick had given strict instructions he was not to leave the house.

Rio's voice purred over the phone, 'I am naked and horny and I *never* take no for an answer. My friends are naked and horny and very very willing to do anything your little heart desires. They are also *very* impressed with your advance publicity, I showed them the pictures, pictures that I'm sure you wouldn't want Daddy to see. Come on over *now*, baby. Bye-bye.'

She hung up and Angelo bit on his thumb nervously.

He had wanted to go and now he had to go.

The only problem was getting out.

The only problem was getting in.

More than anyone Mary Ann August realised how heavily guarded the house was. She had lived there all those months and she knew Enzio's stringent methods for keeping strangers out.

However, she was banking on the fact that she wasn't a stranger. She was Enzio's girlfriend, his mistress. She had gone to New York with him just over a week before and it was perfectly logical that she had come back with him. She did not think Enzio would have bothered to announce the fact that he was sending her away. Enzio would have told Alio, had him do the dirty work, but apart from that—well, she just felt she knew him well enough to know that he kept things to himself.

She had a plan. It was risky. But with luck and with guys she knew on the gate, things might just work out.

'I'm going to the airport,' Nick said.

'Hey, I'll go with you,' Angelo saw a way out. Drive to the airport with his brother and then get conveniently lost.

'No,' Nick shook his head, 'you stay here and take over from me. We don't know what their next move is.'

Angelo hesitated. He didn't want to argue with Nick, but then again he had to get out.

Nick was already on his way to the door, when Angelo decided it would probably be simpler to split when Nick wasn't there anyway.

Chapter 43

Enzio woke about five. His bedroom over-looked the pool, and when he got up he sat by the window and stared out for a while.

He felt very old and tired. A feeling he was not used to. In two months' time he would be seventy years old. Frank had been only thirty-six and they had killed him, a man in his prime, a Bassalino.

Enzio swore quietly to himself, a slow murmuring of never-ending words. A prayer of obscenities.

He would have liked to have gone to Rose, she was the only one who could possibly understand the pain that he felt.

He knew it was impossible. Rose had sworn

never to talk to him again, and he knew Rose, he knew she never would.

Perhaps he should visit the girl he had found in New York—the one Kosta Gennas had brought him—what was her name? Mabel, no, Miriam, that was it, Miriam. She had been sent to the house and installed in the usual room, but so far Enzio had not visited her.

'Filth!' he spat on the floor. They were all filth these women he could buy. Besides which he could summon no sexual interest. At his age it was becoming more difficult.

He lay once more on his bed, perhaps he would sleep some more, perhaps he would feel better in a while.

Images of Frank as a child kept flashing before him. The day he lost his first tooth. The day he learned to swim. The time he beat up a boy at school twice his size. The time Enzio took him to his first girl, Frank thirteen years old. Enzio chuckled, his eyes swam with tears.

The door to his room opened quietly, and for a moment Enzio couldn't quite make out who it was standing there. Then he saw it was Mary Ann August, blonde, beehived hair, small red bikini, long legs and mammoth breasts.

'Hello, sweetie pie,' she said, smiling nicely.

Enzio grunted, and struggled to sit up. Hadn't he sent her away? Hadn't Alio been supposed to deal with her?

Mary Ann swayed towards the bed, 'How's mommy's big bad man?' she cooed, at the same time she undid the tie on her bikini top and her breasts tumbled out.

Enzio's mind was muddled, Alio must have screwed up. Anyway, so what? Mary Ann August was just what he needed now. She knew what he liked, she knew his fads and fancies.

Suddenly he wasn't an old man of nearly seventy, he was a Bassalino, a stud.

She reached the bed and leaned over him, her breasts dangling tantalisingly over his face. He opened his mouth and attempted to cram an obliging nipple in.

She giggled, and he felt her fiddling with his clothes. He closed his eyes and sighed as he felt the erection beginning.

His mouth was full of her when she shot him precisely and silently straight through the heart.

Chapter 44

Angelo left the house soon after Nick. It was easy. Just walk on out, into the black Mustang, drive to the gates, wave at the guards there as they let him through. Easy.

After all, he was a Bassalino too, so who dared question him?

He clicked on the radio. Bobby Womack. Great. He felt good, a little bit high, just enough. The thing with Frank had unnerved him. A fucking bomb right in the middle of New York, that was a hell of a way to go. But he couldn't pretend he was heartbroken. OK. Sure. So Frank was his brother. But he had always been a mean bastard, there had never been any love lost between the two of them.

The thought of seeing Rio again elated him.

She was sending for *him*. It wasn't him phoning or grovelling for a chance to prove himself. *She* wanted *him*. She had tracked *him* down, and flown to Miami specially to see *him*.

Angelo put his foot down a little harder on the accelerator, mustn't keep her waiting, she had said she was waiting.

He turned the radio louder. The disc jockey was talking, rhythmic slang and then loud and clear, James Brown. Sexy, sexy, sexy.

Angelo couldn't help laughing. James Brown would always remind him of his first scene with Rio. 'Sex Machine' had been the record then. He turned the radio full volume so the sound flooded all around him completely deafening. He revved the car and shoved his foot down to the floor.

'Rio baby,' he shouted, 'here I come!'

He failed to see the stop sign ahead and the car plunged through the junction and straight into a truck.

Angelo was killed instantly, but on the car radio James Brown sang on . . .

Chapter 45

'Hey,' Nick gripped her by the arms and stared intently at her.

Lara smiled. 'You came to the airport.'

'Couldn't wait any longer. Has anyone ever told you that you are the most beautiful woman in the world?'

'I love you, Nick. That's why I came.'

'Hey, here's a lady who don't mince words.' He kissed her. 'I love you too, princess. You got any suitcases?'

She nodded, 'One.'

He took her hand and held it tightly, and they walked slowly through the terminal to wait for the suitcases.

'Look,' Nick said, 'there's a lot of things I want to tell you.'

'There's a lot of things I *have* to tell you, Nick.'

'OK, great. We have all the time in the world. Right?'

'Right.'

He stopped walking and pressed his hands around her face and kissed her, a long slow kiss. 'Good to see you, ladybird. We'll go back to the house, you'll meet the family. It's all very heavy at the moment, I don't even want to start explaining. I just want you near me. Is that OK with you?'

Lara nodded. It was fine with her, it was all she wanted. Thank God he was all right. She had to warn him about Dukey. Tell him the whole story. And when he knew, then what? Would he still want her to be near him, or would that be it?

She sighed, it was the only way. Here was the only man she had ever felt anything real for, and to have any kind of relationship with him the truth had to be told.

'There's my suitcase,' she said.

Nick signalled a porter and they set off for the car.

Chapter 46

Mary Ann August left Enzio's room quietly. Outside his door was the suitcase she had packed neatly with her possessions. She had found everything exactly where she had left them. There had been no problem getting into the house, she had just strolled through the grounds in her bikini as though she still lived there.

She wasn't sure why she decided to shoot Enzio. It had just all seemed so easy, the little gun that he had given her for her own protection was still in her jewellery case.

He was such a bastard. Leaving her in New York. Sending Alio along to take his turn. Shipping her off to a whorehouse in Los

Angeles as if she were a side of beef. Keeping all her things.

Now that it was done she started to shake.

What if she couldn't get away?

What if someone *found* him before she could escape?

She hurried down the passage, and then to her horror, as she was about to pass his wife's room, the door opened and the woman called Rose appeared.

She had *never* left her room. Mary Ann had lived in the house for months, and she knew that the door was never opened.

Rose stepped into the hall and they faced each other.

Rose had matted black hair, and shining, insane eyes, and she smiled at Mary Ann, a strange, faraway smile, and then she lifted the knife she was carrying and plunged it into Mary Ann's stomach.

The girl slid to the floor silently and Rose drew the long knife out of her body and continued along the passage to Enzio's room.

He was asleep in bed, the covers drawn tightly round his chin.

Rose started to laugh as she plunged the knife into him.

Plunge, laugh, plunge, laugh.

It was the same knife they had used so many years ago on Charles Cardwell.

Chapter 47

It was nearly five when Leroy parked his Mercedes some distance away from the Bassalino mansion. He was beginning to feel tired, it had been a long day.

He stepped from the car and stretched, at the same time he took stock of his surroundings. There was no one around, no one to observe him.

Most of the work had been done on his last trip. With Enzio away in New York, it had been a relatively simple matter to gain access to the house posing as a telephone engineer. The oldest trick in the world, but when the telephone went dead it always worked. Cut the wires, wait twenty minutes, then appear. 'Telephone engineer, fault reported on your line.'

Guards check the phone, check Leroy's phony credentials, nod agreement that he can come in. At first someone follows him everywhere, but then they get bored and Leroy is on his own.

The place was set up beautifully, only the finishing touches were needed.

Leroy opened the boot of his car and took out a small canvas holdall. He opened it, scanned the contents, and then set off for the house.

* * *

'Christ! We've been sitting here forever,' Nick exclaimed, 'goddamn traffic.'

They were crawling along on a four-lane highway, every lane clogged up.

'It's usually no more than half an hour to the house,' Nick said to Lara. 'Today we'll be lucky to make it in two hours.'

He lit a cigarette impatiently. He should have waited for Lara at the house, it was stupid to have left. There might be news, things might be moving, information might be coming through.

'There's an accident up ahead,' the driver said, 'looks like a bad one. Once we're past that it'll be clear.'

'Thank Christ for that,' Nick clutched at Lara's hand, 'soon be home, baby.'

* * *

Leroy strolled towards the gates of the Bassalino mansion. He paused several yards away. One of the guards stepped out of the side house and watched Leroy warily.

Leroy dipped slowly into his pocket.

'Yeah?' the guard started to question as his hand tightened on a pistol stuck in his belt.

In one moment Leroy produced a hand grenade from his pocket, deftly removed the pin, and threw it at the guardhouse. At the end moment he flung himself flat on the ground, and he felt the earth shake from the explosion.

He counted to five, leaped up, grabbed his canvas bag and ran past the flames into the grounds of the house.

He ran fast, dodging and weaving through the trees.

He could see the house, front door open, men running out waving guns. Lot of white mothers. Didn't know what had hit them.

Leroy dodged round to the back of the house under the cover of the trees. Nobody had spotted him, nobody had even thought to let the dogs free.

Leroy dodged forward to the back window. It took him less than minutes to dig up wires that were buried there, attach them, light them, two would trigger off the rest.

Sonofabitch, what a clever scheme from a

black man. Get moving, Leroy, never cut it too fine.

He started to run from the house.

Zero. One. Two. Three. Four. Five. Pow! First explosion, and at intervals of three seconds, individual explosions all around the house.

Then he realised his mistake. He realised it when he saw the frightened Alsatians running in his direction.

His blue canvas bag. He had left it by the house on the ground, and in it was the fresh steak he had bought for the dogs.

Chapter 48

Cass Long was alone when she saw the news on television.

Her first reaction was of an almost satisfied shock. Then the horror of the whole event shook her as the television cameras wavered in a helicopter above the wreck that had once been the Bassalino mansion.

The scene was one of devastation and horror. Fire still burning, police and firemen swarming all over the place. A row of blanket-covered victims lined up by the swimming pool.

'It has still not been established,' the newscaster said, 'how many bodies are still to be recovered from the house. However, they seem pretty certain that there are more to come,' he paused as whispered information was relayed to him. 'It appears that a series of bombs were placed around the house, triggered to go off at short intervals, we will have more to say on that later. Enzio Bassalino was a well-known figure in Chicago in the twenties, along with his contemporaries Al Capone and Legs Diamond. In recent years he has lived in seclusion and retirement at the house in Miami with . . .'

Cass clicked the television off. She stared at a framed photograph of Margaret hanging on the wall.

It was time to take up Margaret's work again. It was time to go out in the world and do the things that Margaret had been trying to do.

Cass knew who she could turn to.

Chapter 49

Lara would always remember the fear and the pain and the panic of that afternoon with Nick.

They were less than minutes from the house when the explosions started.

'What is it?' Lara had asked. It was a noise like long rumbling peals of thunder.

'Jesus Christ!' Nick muttered, 'move this fucking car,' he screamed at the driver.

Then they saw the smoke and closer the flames. And as they approached the drive Nick said, 'Turn the car round, take her back to the airport. Put her on a plane.'

He jumped from the car and ran towards the house. It was a nightmare scene.

'Nick!' Lara screamed after him, 'come back,

please come back . . . I must tell you, I must tell
you . . .'

The driver had already turned the car
around and they were racing off in the other
direction.

'Nick,' Lara sobbed, 'Nick . . .'

The driver took her to the airport and put
her on a plane to New York.

She was numb.

She went straight to Cass's apartment. Rio
was there and then shortly after Dukey arrived.

He smiled at everyone. He was smoking a
cigar. He looked different. 'We did it my way,'
he stated.

Rio spat at him. '*Your* way. You make me
sick.'

'Results,' Dukey said, 'results are all that
matter.'

'You bastard!' Lara said.

'Why don't you call me a black bastard you
toffee-nosed little cunt.'

Cass said, 'All those other people, all those
innocent people.'

'Fuck it girl,' Dukey said. 'Margaret was
worth every one ten times again.'

Rio shook her head. 'You just don't understand, Margaret wouldn't have wanted any of
this. All Margaret would have wanted was for
what she was doing to be carried on. Her work.'

'Well I wanted revenge. And baby I got it.
Every one of those Bassalino pigs dead. Every
mothafuckin' one!'

* * *

Lara went back to her apartment. Slowly, methodically, she packed up all her things. She was through crying, there were no more tears left.

She didn't know where she would go, what she would do.

When the phone rang she was tempted not to pick it up, it was probably Prince Alfa.

Listlessly she said, 'Hello.'

'Princess? That you? Thank Christ you got out.'

'Nick! You're all right. You're safe!'

'Look, I can't talk. What a mess it is here, you wouldn't believe how terrible . . . I'm with the detectives. Jesus, Lara. My mother, father, my whole family . . . Even Angelo got it in a car smash . . .' He started to choke up. 'I'll call you again tomorrow, wait for me sweetheart.'

'I'll fly back, I'll come to you.'

'No. Stay where you are, princess. I'l be with you as soon as I can.'

She could never tell him. No way. But at least he was not harmed, and they would be together. Maybe one day in five years or ten, she would tell him the whole story. Maybe . . .

Chapter 50

Bosco Sam and Dukey K. Williams met at the zoo.

'I ain't truckin' with you past those goddamn monkeys again!' Dukey complained. 'I'm still smelling monkey piss every time I wear my mink coat!'

Bosco Sam heaved with laughter.

'What's the spiel?' Dukey asked. 'Lay it on me, brother, I gotta be at rehearsal two hours ago. Little blonde number held me up.'

'Dukey, boy, we had a deal.'

'Right on. Ain't nobody arguing that fact.'

Bosco Sam produced a bar of chocolate from his coat pocket, and slowly peeled off the wrapper. 'Deal was I forget the two hundred thou—

and you arrange the killings of the Bassalinos. Right?'

'OK Frank Bassalino I give you. But the others?'

'Look, Enzio was the important one—right? Leroy did a great job.'

'Leroy got his ass chewed off by a pack of fuckin' wild hounds. What was left of him his own mother wouldn't recognise. I saw the police photos. I got *very fine* connections with the fuzz.'

'So?'

'So Enzio was got at before the house blew. Shot right through the heart and sliced up with a knife just for fun. You getting it?'

Dukey licked his lips, 'Not really.'

'Angelo Bassalino got his in a car wreck. Nick Bassalino's safe and sound back in Los Angeles. I reckon that still leaves you one-hundred-and-fifty thousand in my debt.'

'Now come on man, you don't mean . . .'

Bosco Sam interrupted. 'With interest we'll call it a straight two-hundred thousand. Two days, Dukey. I'll give you two days.'

'Come on, man,' Dukey pleaded, 'that just ain't fair . . .'

'Fair? Fair? I've been very fair with you. I don't have to tell you what happens next. Two days is generous.'

'You fucker!' Dukey exclaimed, 'even at school you were jealous of me. You fat little fucker! You'll get your money.'

Bosco Sam nodded. 'Sure I will, Dukey boy. Sure I will. Cash. By six o'clock tonight.' Abruptly he shoved the chocolate in his mouth and walked away.

Dukey started to sweat.

There was no way he could get two-hundred thousand together by six o'clock. No way.

Chapter 51

'The guy who comes to you with his cock hanging out may want to fuck you, but does he want to work next to you? Does he want to see you get paid the same money for the same job as he's doing? Hey there—what about the cat in the street who undresses you with his eyes, fucks you with his mouth to his friends—he your equal, baby? Well?'

The crowd of females joined by most of their male friends at the pop festival screamed their agreement with what Rio Java was saying.

'Hey, females—you want to be put down by a race of male pigs for ever? *Old* pigs with racist, chauvinistic, biased, old-fashioned views on *everything* that affects women in America today.

'To them we are but pieces of ass. Look pretty, have the kids, but baby—stay home or stay quiet.'

She was speaking between appearances of pop groups. With her frizzy purple hair and sequinned make-up, she looked like a pop star herself.

In one year she had become as dedicated and intense as Margaret Lawrence Brown ever was. And her following was just as large, in fact, she attracted an even wider group of supporters than Margaret, as even the freaks liked her.

'One day I'm going to be President,' Rio had told anyone who would listen. 'And I am going to expose the whole stinking corrupt mess that politics represents.'

'For a start,' she told her friends, 'I am going to expose that sonofabitch Larry Bolding. He ain't gonna be running for nothin' when I get through with him.'

Larry Bolding, with the clean-cut image, pretty, blonde, elegant wife, and two perfect little kiddies, was running as a Presidential candidate.

Rio held both arms straight up above her purple hair and made fists of her hands.

'Strike out, sisters!' she shouted. 'Strike out!! We are going to get *in* there.'

The crowd whistled and screamed approval.

Rio felt the bullet hit her, but she still stood, she still smiled, and the crowd spread out before her still whistled and, stamped and screamed.

'Strike out!' Rio managed. But then the blood bubbled up her throat and out of her mouth, in one lifetaking gush.

The house in Connecticut could be approached only by going through electronically controlled gates, and then passing the scrutiny of two uniformed guards with pistols stuck casually in their belts.

Dickson Grade passed this scrutiny easily. He was a neat, precise man, in a dark business suit, and he wore rimless glasses on small brown eyes.

He approached the big house, holding a slim briefcase tightly to his side.

A black-uniformed maid answered his ring at the door. 'Good afternoon, Mr Grade. Mr Bolding is out by the pool.'

Dickson Grade nodded slightly and made his way through the house to the patio which led on to an olympic-size swimming pool.

Susan Bolding greeted him. She was a most attractive woman, with straight blonde hair pulled firmly back in a neat bun. Her shapely figure was concealed beneath a loose silk shirt and white trousers.

'Hello, Dick,' she smiled and kissed him lightly on the cheek. 'What can I get you? A drink? Tea? Coffee?'

Dickson nodded politely, he found Larry

Bolding's wife extremely appealing, but when you were Larry Bolding's personal assistant you sat on thoughts like that and did nothing about them.

'Coffee, please, Susan. Where is Larry?'

'Exploring the garden in search of weeds I think. Honestly, Sunday is the only day he even gets time to see it.'

'I'll go find him.'

Dickson walked off down a side path until he found Larry Bolding playing on the grass with his children.

They greeted each other, and then Larry sent the children off to find 'Mommy'. He was a tall, clean-cut man in his early forties. Craggy good looks, deep masculine voice, a politician's firm, gripping handshake.

'Everything is under control,' Dickson said, 'a perfect operation.'

'Is she—dead?'

Dickson nodded, 'And nothing to connect it with us. You're in the clear. Also the right people will be dealing with her personal effects.'

Larry Bolding sighed, and patted Dickson on the shoulder. 'It was the only way, wasn't it?'

Dickson Grade nodded agreement, 'The only way.'